D0102368
crush
LANCASHIRE COUNTY LIBRARY
30118132760160

To Tom. No words. Just so much love. x

Scholastic Children's Books
An imprint of Scholastic Ltd
Euston House, 24 Eversholt Street, London, NW1 1DB, UK

Registered office: Westfield Road, Southam, Warwickshire, CV47 0RA
SCHOLASTIC and associated logos are trademarks and/or
registered trademarks of Scholastic Inc.

First published in the UK by Scholastic Ltd, 2016

ISBN 978 1407 14690 4

A CIP catalogue record for this book
is available from the British Library.

Printed by CPI Group (UK) Ltd, Croydon, CR0 4YY
Papers used by Scholastic Children's Books are made
from wood grown in sustainable forests.

1 3 5 7 9 10 8 6 4 2

www.scholastic.co.uk

Crush

Eve Ainsworth

SCHOLASTIC

I met him on the second of May. It's not like I could ever forget that date. It was my brother's tenth birthday.

It was the also the day I started counselling at school. I didn't want to go, not really. I was suspicious of the small room at the back of the main building. The room with the smiley-face sticker on the door. Jeez, it was so primary school. Only the kids with the problems went in there. The screw-ups. The ones who sobbed in class because they couldn't cope – those types. Not me. Never me.

Didn't they know I hated talking? I slumped in the thick leather chair and tried hard not to look at the woman in front of me. She told me her name was Debbie, Debs for short. She held out a small, white hand – which I ignored. She didn't seem to mind. She did a soft laugh thing and sat back in her own seat like she was so relaxed and chilled out about the whole thing. I kept looking at her shoes, pointy red high heels. Expensive, I reckoned, possibly designer.

She talked for a bit about counselling. About her. About the school. I muttered stuff back just to fill the gaps. I didn't like the silences, they unnerved me, made me more aware that she was busy looking at me – trying to figure me out. I glanced at her, noticing how carefully made up her face was. She was pretty in an old sort of way. She had lines round her mouth and saggy cheeks; make-up just couldn't hide that.

"Is there anything you want to talk about, Anna?"

Her voice was soft and sweet, like sugary candyfloss – her words hanging uselessly between us. I could almost picture them in mid-air, sticky and light, waiting for me to taste them, accept them. But I never did, of course. I continued to sit and stare at my hands. They were folded neatly in my lap, pale and small, almost lost in the folds of my school skirt. I decided I hated her eyes. They creeped me out. They were too small, too blue – like a rabbit's. I imagined her nibbling on a carrot, still staring at me. Waiting for me to answer.

"I can't help you if you don't talk to me." She sighed. A burst of sharp air.

It didn't help that the room was really enclosed, like the inside of a shoebox. It was painted light grey and above her head was a painting, pink and yellow swirls, looking like weird, bent-out-of-shape wheels, someone's drugged-up dream. There was only a tiny window, a small slice of light which seemed to cut her legs in half.

I shuffled a little. The seat, although it looked soft at first, was actually really uncomfortable. My bum was feeling heavy and numb. There was no clock in here, but I was sure we must be near the end of school. This couldn't drag on for ever.

She sighed again, pushing a loose strand of blonde hair behind her ear, a bit that managed to escape her tightly pulled ponytail. Otherwise every inch of her was controlled and managed. She rustled through the folder that sat on her lap, the notes that told her everything about me. Or at least, she thought they did.

"Can you at least tell me a little bit about your dad?" she said. "How are things at home? Now, it's just you, him and your brother, isn't it?"

"Yes," I said, bluntly.

"And you get on OK?"

I shrugged. "Fine. It's fine."

I flicked my eyes away from hers, hating this so much.

"And your mum. . . ?"

"No!" My hands clenched, fingernails gripping the skin. "No, not her. I don't talk about her."

"OK. No problem. Maybe that's something we can touch on another time," she said.

I nod. Or maybe not. . .

"You understand why I wanted to talk to you though?"

"I guess."

"You were referred by your form teacher. She worries that you've been more upset than usual. Very quiet in class. Distracted, maybe?"

I felt myself burning. I needed to get out of here. The room was too small; my legs were buzzing with the stress from sitting still. Outside the sun was streaming. I wanted to be there, in the air, not talking. I remembered the times in lessons when I felt so wound up, for nothing really. I pictured myself slamming my hand against the wall and yelling out in frustration. I'd never done it, but I'd wanted to. A lot.

"Sometimes," I said.

"Well, obviously the school were concerned enough to refer you. They seem to think you might be struggling a bit. Do you think that's true?"

"Sometimes," I said again.

"It's nothing to be frightened of, Anna. I'm not the bad guy here. I just want to try and help."

I nodded. I stared at her eyes again, brighter now – more pressing. I wanted to sort out some of the bad stuff inside me, feelings that swirled around me like a negative storm. If she helped with that I would be happy. Just nothing else. I wasn't up for talking.

She smiled. "That's good, then. Obviously this is totally voluntary. If you're not up for it – well, that's fine."

"I'm not."

"It's just – well, if you ever want to talk about things. Stuff about your mum, for example. . ."

I rolled my eyes. How thick was she?

"It's normal to miss her," she said.

"I don't."

"I can understand why you might feel angry towards her."

I stood up then. I didn't mean to, but her words

were hammering into my head, hitting old bruises. I didn't want this. I didn't ask for this.

"I want to go now," I said. As if on cue, the bell sounded. My signal to leave.

Debs stared up, her cool eyes unblinking. "I understand. Maybe you're not ready?"

"I don't need to talk about it."

"Just so I know, do you have anyone you can talk to?"

"I don't need to," I said again. Was she thick? Or deaf?

"Everyone needs someone."

I picked up my bag and turned. I felt sluggish, like I needed to sleep. The room was killing me, sapping every inch of me.

"But, Anna," she said, sitting forward and handing me a small card. "I'm here for you when you're ready for me. Maybe we can meet every week or so? Just to see how things are going? If you don't want to go into stuff, that's fine."

"Maybe," I muttered.

I walked out, not bothering to turn back.

I didn't go home, not straight away. My head was beginning to ache. I needed to walk, get some space.

So I kept moving, swung out of the school gates and turned down the main road.

I knew Dad wanted me home on time. I should've been there blowing up balloons for Eddie – making a big fuss of my stupid brother. I think I did start out heading that way, but something made me walk straight past the bus stop. I just kept walking further out of town and towards the Swamp. My iPod earbuds were rammed deep into my ears; music was blasting into me. I guess I knew I couldn't go home yet – I wasn't ready. If I went home in a worse mood than normal, things would be bad.

The Swamp is the poor excuse for a lake that sits on the other side of town. The name Swamp pretty much suits it. The water is made up of mushy mud and skanky reeds. I think I may have seen a fish once, maybe twice. Eddie always says there are bodies in the bottom, maybe some jewels. I think that's unlikely – it's just trash, old cans and rusty pieces of metal. Sometimes it's quiet, other times there are other kids there, swinging on rope from the large looming trees or fishing for junk in the dark waters.

It's somewhere to go, I guess. Some place to be.

When I go there, I sit at the furthest spot, by a broken-down weeping willow, which is not so much weeping as full-on wailing. I think someone must have hacked at the bark once, because it's pretty cut up on one side. Next to it is the stump of another fallen tree. It's a good place to chill. Usually I play music and stare into the swirling mud. I try not to think too much; I want to be able to de-stress. But sometimes my head is so full up, I end up churning everything around – pulling apart the little bits of my life and analysing them. Wondering how I could change them. How I could escape.

That day, I was thinking about Debs, about her beady eyes and shiny red shoes. I was thinking about the small card that I'd shoved into my pocket. My thoughts fluttered to Dad and Eddie at home, getting his party ready. I could picture Dad, stressing over the food. Not getting things right. I felt myself squirm. I knew I should be there.

"Hey."

I jumped instinctively. It was a loud shout. I tugged out my headphones and turned, irritated and embarrassed at being caught sitting there like some sad loner. I expected some kid to be standing there, someone annoying, someone looking for attention. But it wasn't.

It was Will Bennett from Year Eleven, who'd

never even looked in my direction before. And he was holding my purse.

I stared at it, open-mouthed, and then reached inside my pocket. It had gone and I hadn't realized.

"Looking for this?" he said, grinning at me.

I swear I didn't even know how to answer. I mean, it was so weird that he was actually standing there in front of me, let alone holding my purse. This wasn't just any guy, this was the guy every girl at school wanted to be with. I tried to gather myself a bit, feeling queasy inside. I didn't want to look like some uncool freak, all jittery in front of him.

He was smiling at me, in his casual, sexy way. I was trying not to look at him full on, but it was hard not to. I didn't want him to know I was like everyone else. I really didn't want him to know that he had any effect on me. He was only inches away, tall and slim. His cheeks and jaw were so well defined, like they had been carved or sculpted. His hair blond, short against his pale skin. He made me think of ice.

"Do you want it, then?" he said, offering me the purse. "I found it just outside the school gates and saw your lunch card in it."

I felt my cheeks burn. That picture was awful.

"Thank you," I said, taking the purse and brushing his hand as I did. It was weird: the hype around him annoyed me a bit, and he was almost too good-looking, but being so close was unnerving. I felt so . . . well, shy – stupid.

"It's a cute picture," he said.

I laughed then. "Liar. I look awful."

"Did you miss the bus? Is that why you came here?" He looked concerned. I stared up at his face, at his light blue eyes that seemed to sparkle even when he was being serious.

"Not exactly," I said, sitting myself down again. "I just wanted to waste some time, that's all. It's my brother's party today. I'm not sure I can face it."

"Party? Sounds cool."

I shook my head. "It'll be far from cool. My brother is ten and a total freak. We hate each other. My dad thinks he's Mr Wonderful though, so I should to be there – whether I want to or not."

Will laughed. I liked the sound, it was deep and honest. I found myself relaxing. I looked at him again, at his hands, long and slim. At his slender nose. At his lips, curled and not too plump.

"Can I sit with you for a bit? Maybe walk you back to the bus stop when you're ready?" he asked.

"I don't like leaving you on your own. There's some total nutters around, you know."

"Sure." I tried to stay casual, but my heart was beating overtime. I was two years younger than him. I was nothing. Why was he bothered about me?

He sat on the grass opposite me, his legs drawn up in front of him. "So what happens at these parties?" he asked me. He was sitting quite close; in fact our legs were almost touching.

"What happens? Well, my brother will invite his annoying mates. They'll all be quite hyper, stupid and . . . well, just weird. My dad will make loads of fuss of him and I'll hide in my room waiting for it all to be over."

"Sounds fun."

"Yeah, it's great fun." I shook my head. "Seriously, it's like the worst kind of hell."

"Where would you rather be?"

"Anywhere!"

"In a vat of rats?" he asked.

"Any day!" I laughed.

He laughed too. "Actually, I'm glad you dropped your purse," he said softly. "It gave me a chance to come and speak to you."

I could feel myself glowing; then a thought

dawned on me. "How did you know where I would be?"

"I followed you here. Hey, that sounds a bit weird. Like I'm a stalker or something. I'm not. I just saw you drop the purse and saw it as a good time to . . . I dunno, try and talk?" He shifted slightly, pushed his hair back away from his face. "I hope you don't mind?"

"No, I guess not. . ." My stomach was somersaulting inside me.

"I thought maybe you'd be waiting for a bus and maybe we could chat then," he said. "Hey – this sounds so lame. I just think you're really cute."

"Cute?" I think my voice cracked a bit, so naff.

"Yeah – you are – honestly!"

I giggled then, I couldn't help it. Most days I hated the way I looked. Actually – make that every day.

"Don't laugh. I mean it. You're really fit."

His eyes, like droplets of light, were gazing straight into me. It sounded so stupid, but I was softening, melting towards him. How could this have happened so quickly? This wasn't like me. Stuff like this just didn't happen.

My day, my life, had suddenly improved.

It's strange, this, talking to you. But they reckon it will help. They say it will help me deal with stuff. It's worth trying, isn't it – she said.

She told me, that counsellor woman, to pick a person, any person who I want to talk to. I told her 'no one'. She said there must be someone, someone that I have things to say to. She said I can talk aloud. Or write. I don't even have to send it anywhere – I can just screw it up and throw it away. Or burn it. Whatever. So I thought, what the hell – it's worth a shot. It might get this crap out of my head.

I picked you, because—

I dunno. I just picked you.

They say I might need help. I don't think so. I'm just stressed you're not here, that's all. You got away. Everything has changed now, but you wouldn't know that, would you? You don't realize what you caused.

I'm angry because of you. Because of Mum flipping out again. Because of ALL OF IT. I feel it throughout my body – like all the switches have been turned on. It buzzes through me like an electric current. I guess I feel more alive, more aware of stuff.

Most days Mum struggles to get out of bed.

I can't even talk to her. It's not allowed. We have to whisper. Treat her like a fragile piece of . . . what? Junk?

You wouldn't put up with that, would you? Then again, I'm sure she wasn't this bad around you? You don't know the half of it.

I could slap Mum round the face and she'd just take it, suck it up. She always does. I just want to yell in her pale stupid face.

So yeah, I'm stressed.

What's new?

Will.

He isn't going to show up. No way. This is some kind of twisted joke. Yeah, that would be typical of my luck. Serves me right for even daring to believe it.

I kept glancing around me, expecting Dan to jump out at any second and laugh right in my face. It would just be like him to set me up like this.

I'll give him five minutes, that's all... Any more and it proves he's not really interested. I mean, honestly, why would he be? This is Will Bennett after all. You silly cow. He couldn't really be interested in you. You're, like, nothing to him. Nothing.

Will Bennett ... jeez ... seriously?

I was sat on the tree stump again, staring out at the brown sludge – trying hard to decide whether the glistening thing I could see in the water was some kind of creature, or maybe a plant? My feet were digging at the loose dirt around me, trailing circles in the brown dust. I felt so on edge, it was like every nerve inside me was on fire. It had been three days since we swapped numbers, just three days and he was already doing my head in.

"So, what you staring at, then?"

He seemed to come out from nowhere, silently up the dried mud track. My whole body lurched. Something sparked down my spine. I felt a bit sick too. I wasn't used to this. Boys were mates to me, people I hung around with, had a laugh with. They didn't make me feel all quivery and naff.

"That out there." I pointed wildly. "I'm trying to work out if it's a fish."

Will stood right behind me and kind of ducked down, so I could feel him against me. He had a lovely fresh smell. I tried hard not to be obvious and breathe it in like a crazy freak.

"Nah. Not a fish."

I looked again. Squinting this time. It was definitely shiny. "You don't think?" I shifted, feeling silly now.

"I'd say it's the back of a supermarket trolley."

Of course; now I could see it was a metal bar of some sort. I was blushing. Trust me to think it was alive. "Maybe I need glasses," I said.

"Maybe you need to learn what fish look like." Will was laughing. "I love fishing. Maybe you could come sometime."

He stepped back and I turned to face him. He was looking good. Even though he was wearing a school uniform like me, he seemed casual somehow. Maybe it was because he'd taken his tie off and loosened his shirt. His hair was more messy and springing about. As if he was reading my mind, his hand reached up and attempted to flatten it.

"Shall we go for a walk?" he said.

I nodded. I felt myself blush again as he took my hand in his. I still wanted to shake myself to believe it was actually happening.

"You look nervous," he said as we made our way down the path.

"I guess I am a bit." I tried to keep my words steady. "I guess I want to make a good impression."

"Why wouldn't you? You look great."

My stomach flipped and seemed to be slivering inside of me, like a twitching snake. I tried not to grip his hand too hard but I really wanted to. I wanted to squeeze him so tight and keep him close. Surely this wasn't going to last for long? He was bound to see sense soon. I had to enjoy it while I could. I had to remember this bit for ever.

It might be gone tomorrow.

We followed the path round the Swamp, not much of a walk really, but the one that most dog walkers took. At this time of day it was surprisingly quiet. The trees were a protective barrier against the late afternoon sun, throwing flashes of light and shade against us as we walked. The shadows seemed to be dancing as we moved through them, sparkles from the water shimmering beside us.

"I'm glad you met me. I was scared you wouldn't show," he said. "I could see me standing here by myself, like some miserable loner."

He felt like that? For real?

I smiled and shook my head. He gripped my hand tighter.

"I saw you at the school concert, in that band – what's it called?"

"Void," I said, feeling myself glow. "You saw us?"

"Yeah. You were amazing. Your voice. Seriously, I think that's when I first saw you. Like *really* saw you. . ."

The school concert had been months ago. The thought of Will being there and noticing me was pretty amazing.

"Did you like the music?" I asked, as we picked our way over fallen branches that lay in the path.

"Yeah. It was OK. Bit intense – but OK."

I laughed again. I could tell he was trying to be nice. Void played pretty heavy, dark stuff. Mainly down to my mate Dan, who played guitar and wrote most of the songs. He liked to think that intense, "clever" music would attract girls, and to be fair, it seemed to work for him.

"Well. I'm glad you liked it," I said.

"After that, I kept seeing you in the corridors and stuff. I'd smile, but I don't think you saw. I'm just glad you dropped your purse. It gave me the perfect opportunity."

I smiled. "I never thought you'd be shy to talk to someone. Why didn't you come up and say hi or something?"

Will shrugged. "I don't know. I'm not normally shy, but you're a bit different. You come across quite – I don't know, guarded?"

"I'm fussy with who I spend my time with," I said. "I've got no time for losers."

"I'm not a loser," he said in mock protest.

"Good. I'm glad to hear that," I teased.

We stopped walking. We were standing right

beneath a large oak tree, its branches extending right over the Swamp. It seemed to engulf us. A wooden protector.

"I bet he's been here for ever," I said, patting the bark.

"Seen a lot of things," Will agreed. "One day I'll carve our names into the bark."

"No, don't! You'll hurt the tree!"

"OK. I'll paint them on. Would that be OK?"

I nodded. "Yeah, fine. One day you can do that."

"One day." He smiled and traced his finger over the trunk, lingering for a while. It was like our names were already there – intertwined together – Will and Anna.

Together. Seriously weird.

He bent forward. His lips just brushed mine at first. He eased away a bit and stared at me, like he was checking it was OK. It was OK, it really was. His mouth met mine again, but this time harder, more urgent. His hands gripped my arms. His tongue gently stroked the inside of my lips, slipped further inside my mouth – all the time he was kind of pulling me towards him. I could taste his warmth, could feel the slight roughness of his skin against mine.

As we drew apart, he gasped a little. "I really want to see you again."

"Yes," I said, staring up at his blue eyes. I felt like they were sparkling just for me.

"Soon," he whispered.

And he kissed me again. And again.

He walked me to the bus stop about an hour later. I felt like my lips were on fire, so swollen and sore. But that didn't matter. It didn't matter at all.

There was no one else around. He reached forward and gently pulled my hair out from behind my ears. He played with the strands, winding them between his fingers like they were silk.

"You look beautiful with your hair down," he said. "You should always wear it like that, don't scrape it back."

I wanted to giggle. My hair was the biggest stress of my life – so thick and unruly. Most of the time I wanted to hack it all off, except I was paranoid it would make me look even younger. I remember my mum trying so hard to tame it into shape when I was young. She used to curse under her breath as she tried to brush out the curls. I'd look at her own long blonde ponytail and want to cry with envy.

"I always tie it up," I muttered, shy again.

"Don't." He was smiling. His fingers seemed to be dancing across my scalp, freeing my curls. "Please don't."

Inside me that snake was twitching again, slivering in the pit of my stomach, making it twist and flip. I think I was shaking a little. It was all unreal. I was waiting to snap awake. My life had never been like this. I just went home and sat in my room, singing alone to the walls. No boy had registered me before. I was a nothing.

Until now.

"This was good," he said softly. "I loved being with you today."

I grinned, truly naff, but I couldn't help myself. "So did I!"

"Let's do much more of this," he said, bringing my face towards his. All I could do was nod numbly as his lips found mine again.

I barely noticed the bus arrive. I barely noticed anything.

Just us.

I strode up the stairs that led to our flat. Twelve storeys. That's two hundred and sixteen steps.

I should know; I counted them every day. I knew that the tenth step had a blob of chewing gum on it, the shape of Ireland. I knew the twenty-second step was stained and dark. The fortieth step had graffiti on it – just initials, a T and a twisted-up S. I hadn't got a clue who would be bored enough to draw on a step, but there was obviously some sad freak out there.

To me, each step was musical, a gentle rhythm, more beats that added to the stuff in my head. Music never left me; it was always there. I sang softly under my breath.

"Now it's just us two, I know

The pain of never letting you go…"

Dan's lyrics were often stuck in my head, dancing around my brain like a trapped animal. Even when I had other stuff going on, I couldn't stop the tune flooding in. I knew I'd got this bit right now – the bit I'd struggled with for days. It was sounding good and I couldn't wait to sing it to him at rehearsals tomorrow. Having "head music" made the climb a bit easier. The lifts had been out of action so many times, I should have been used to it. Men came and fixed them, spent days behind taped yellow barriers, and in a matter of hours sometimes, it all got smashed up again.

Not that I minded really. I avoided the lifts even when they were working. They were horrible, smelly metal traps.

I reached the last flight and my breath was turning into a dry, raspy cough. I paused in the narrow corridor, blinking in the dim light. I hated living there. I guessed Dad did too; why else would he send me to a school half an hour away? He always said I could "do better", that my "brains would lead me anywhere I wanted".

Yeah, right. . .

I pushed my key in the lock and gently eased the door open. The room was thick with gangster lyrics coming from Eddie's docking station.

"I'm back!" I yelled over the noise.

As usual, the room was full of Eddie's mates, lounging over the chairs, shouting at the Xbox. Eddie was on the floor, always the loudest. He took one look at me and flicked his middle finger up.

I walked past him, into the kitchen. Dad had his back to me. He was busy stirring a curry. "You're late," he said, his voice flat.

"I'm sorry."

"I told you not to be late. You were meant to be cooking."

"I said, I'm sorry. I missed the bus."

I couldn't tell him I was with Will. I couldn't tell him that kissing some boy was more important than cooking and cleaning in this stupid flat.

Dad sighed but didn't turn. "Well, you finish this off and then you can clean up the mess." He walked out of the room without even looking at me.

Except this time, I couldn't stop the smile that crept back on to my face, just thinking of Will. I turned to the oven and the softly bubbling pan. I picked up the spoon, stained yellow by the thick sauce, and began to stir. More words flowed. I sang softly into the steam.

Most evenings were the same.

But this time I was singing to Will.

So I guess I'm not feeling so bad at the moment. It's also because I'm not at home much. Last night I stayed with Zak. The night before I was out late and slipped over the back gate like you used to.

Mum is more or less spaced out these days. She's crying a lot. Sometimes she shouts. I've given up trying to talk to her. She never listens to me anyway. She looks at me like I'm not really there.

It's been almost four years since you left. Two weeks before my birthday.

I never got a card – from you or her – that year.

It's my seventeenth birthday in two months and I bet they'll forget again this year. In fact, I'd lay money on it.

Most years I remind her. I'm not sure I'll bother this time.

I had two best mates at school. Izzy, who I'd known pretty much since primary school, and Dan, from the band. I'd not known Dan as long, only since Year Seven, but we hit it off from the first week at St Nick's. We both loved music and appreciated good sounds. Sometimes we'd write music together, but my lyrics were never as good as his. Never as deep. I didn't like that sort of music until I met him. I'd pretty much grown up on R&B and hip hop, but suddenly I found myself listening to indie rock. I guess it alienated me from Dad and Eddie even more.

Dan was my talented friend, the one I felt slightly in awe of. But Izzy was my sunshine, the one to gossip with, my source of fun.

She was the first one I told about Will, the day after our first "date". We sat huddled together at the back of English, pretending to work on our assignments.

"Seriously," she hissed, "he wants to see you again."

I nodded, trying not to look smug or anything. "Yeah. I know. It's crazy."

Izzy shook her head, blonde curls bouncing against her pink cheeks. "This is so big, Anna. I mean, this is Will Bennett. Everyone fancies him. I'm so jealous I would poke your eyes right out – if I didn't love you so much."

"Please don't poke my eyes out."

"I just can't believe it!" Her eyes were so big and bright. "You have to give me all the gossip. Every last detail."

"Of course," I promised.

"Promise?"

As she nudged me, I felt my phone vibrate in my pocket. Even though it was on silent, I shifted uneasily in my seat – paranoid that my super-strict teacher, Mrs Arden, would notice. I expertly eased it out and slid it on to my lap. A message from Will, during lessons. Cheeky.

"Is it him?" Izzy asked, peering over.

"Ssh." I pushed the textbook closer towards us. "Don't make it obvious." Carefully I peered down and used one finger to unlock the screen.

Hey. Can I see you at lunch? Been thinking about you all day (and night) xx

I shivered. Was it nerves or just the pure excitement of reading those words? I pushed the phone between my legs and grinned.

"Well?" Izzy said.

"He wants to see me at lunch." I saw Izzy's expression change a little. If I didn't have rehearsals, that was usually our time, when we would properly catch up and gossip – share crisps and plan out our weekend. "Do you mind?"

Izzy smiled. "Of course not; it's not like it's going to be every day, is it?"

"Of course it won't," I said.

The phone remained sandwiched between my thighs. I didn't dare move it again, but having it there was exciting. His message was there just waiting for me.

I was feeling great.

"You look really pretty today," Will said softly.

"Thank you."

We were sat under the big tree at the back of the school field. It was shady there, cool. Will was sprawled out, long legs stretched out in the long grass. I was more self-conscious and sat on my knees, aware that my skirt rode up, showing off my (slightly chunky) legs. I felt so silly and shy sitting there, like it was all wrong, some kind of joke. I felt like I should have a big sticker on my head: "YOU DON'T BELONG HERE!"

I'd noticed the other girls watching us walk off together. I saw their faces crease in curiosity. Would they be talking about us? Would we be the next source of gossip? Loads of them were still looking over; I could feel their eyes burning in my direction. They must've been talking. They must've been wondering how I had managed to get with Will.

It was crazy weird in my head too.

"Did you mind me texting you?" he asked.

Did I mind?

"No, of course not." I smiled. "I think Mrs Arden might've flipped if she'd noticed though."

"Oh, that old cow," Will sniffed. "I just really wanted to see you again. Couldn't wait till after school."

"Good job you did anyway; I'm meeting the band straight from school."

Will frowned a little. "Really? Aw, that sucks. See, I'll miss you."

"Am I really that irresistible?"

"There's something about you." His hand took mine, started to stroke my fingers. Little tingles of energy sparked down my back, made me want to wriggle – it was so weird. "I dunno what it is but you get right inside my head."

I stared back at him, at his intense gaze – his eyes still twinkling. "Are you like this with all your girlfriends?"

"All my girlfriends?" He looked confused; the stroking stopped. "What do you mean?"

I shrugged. "Well – it's just I've heard that you've dated quite a few girls."

He laughed, softer this time. "No way. Jeez, the gossip in this place drives me mad. I dated one girl for a while. Sophie, in my year? But other than that, no one else. Not really."

I knew who he meant. Sophie Baxter was dead pretty, like turn-your-head gorgeous. A true blonde-haired, blue-eyed beauty – nothing like me. In fact, she was as far from me as you could possibly get. I'd also heard people say she was stuck up, not very friendly. I had no clue if that was true or not – but obviously she and Will had been a pretty glamorous couple.

"Seriously, Anna. I wouldn't just say this. I really

like you. Really like you in a 'you're doing my head in' way."

I nudged him with my elbow. "That sounds harsh. I shouldn't be doing your head in."

"Well, you are. And it's a good thing. So just kiss me and put me out of my misery."

So, in front of most of the school, I did.

My second best mate, Dan, wasn't as interested in my new relationship. I didn't even have to tell him. He'd heard all about it when I walked into the music room.

"Will Bennett, then?" he said, eyebrow raised.

"Yeah. And?"

"No, nothing. I just didn't think he'd be your type," Dan said, fiddling with his guitar. "You know, I thought you'd go for someone with more, I don't know – depth?"

I frowned. "You don't even know him."

"Yeah ... I sort of do. He only lives a few streets away from me. And we went to the same primary. I'd hardly forget that family..."

"What do you mean?"

"Nothing. I mean, nothing. He's cool." He picks up his guitar and mutters something under his breath.

"What was that?" I asked.

"I said – as long as you're happy."

I dumped my stuff in the corner of the room, placing my mobile on top of my bag in case it went off. Will's picture was saved on my phone, one that he'd just sent me. I stared at it for a bit. He looked good in this one: the nub of his cheekbone pressing through his stubbly cheek; his strong, slightly angular jaw; his blond hair contrasting against the shadows. He looked moody, like he often did. Distant. That's why all the girls at school fancied him.

As if on cue, Dan got up and came up behind me. "Nice pic."

I quickly flicked the image away. "Yeah. It is."

Dan had that look on his face, the one he always had when he was in a wind-up mood. His eyes seemed brighter somehow, more alert, ready to attack. "So, you're getting all loved-up then?"

I shrugged. "It's still pretty early days. But I do really like him." I smiled. "Is that OK with you, boss?"

"I guess it's quite amusing that you're dating the King of Cool. I suppose it might do the band good."

"So why were you so grumpy when I walked in?" I couldn't resist nudging him. "Not jealous, are you?"

Dan snorted. "Hardly. I've seen you pick your nose, remember." He screamed as I punched him in the arm. "All right, all right . . . but seriously, it's just, he's a bit . . . you know. . ." He shrugged.

"What?" My cheeks were burning. "What is he?"

"A bit 'look at me, everyone fancies me' – you know. . ." He trailed off.

"And you're not?"

Dan puffed out his chest. "I'm totally different. I have that guitarist cool vibe about me."

I snorted. "Yeah. OK. If you say so!"

"Well, I guess it's good for the music. You can help me move away from the darker stuff. We can write more soppy stuff. Things you girls like. It might help me pull."

I grinned. "Yeah, I can see you loving that!" I shifted away from his gleaming eyes, eager to change the subject. "Come on, we're here to practise. I thought you wanted to go over that line again."

Dan nodded. "Yeah. Yeah I do. Ready when you are."

I shuffled away from him, closed my eyes. I found it easier not to look at people when I sang, even Dan, who I felt like I'd known for ever. Cheeky Dan, long floppy hair and dark blue eyes, never short of attention from the girls, who never knew what an annoying idiot he could be. Chris and Max, the others in the band, hadn't arrived yet, so it was just us in the small, dim music room. Nerves were kicking in and I wanted them to walk in and interrupt. I wanted us all to be messing around as usual.

Instead, I breathed out slowly and let the song come.

"Trust is what I needed now
Only you could show me how...
Why did you destroy this?
Denied your lies. A tainted kiss."

I kept my eyes closed for a few seconds. I was pretty sure I'd got it spot on this time. My voice seemed right – more on pitch, like the words had fitted my mouth. I loved it when this happened. This was when I truly believed I could do it.

I *could* sing. Sing really well.

"That's fab, Anna! You sounded amazing." Dan was behind me. He threw his arms around me, this great bundle of energy, and we both giggled.

"This could be the one!" I said, still giggling.

"The one!" he agreed.

Ever since I joined the band, we joked that we would find a song that would make us a million, make us rock stars, make us famous.

"We're going to do this," I said, thumping his leg in excitement. "We really are."

"With that voice, you could do anything," Dan said. But his face was calmer; he wasn't laughing. "Seriously, Anna. That was awesome. You're awesome."

I shake my head. "No . . . I—"

"You've gotta start believing in yourself. Really," he sighed. "I wish you could see how great you are."

I pushed him away, knowing I was getting hot, uncomfortable. I didn't want to hear all that stuff. I could swear the room was getting smaller somehow. I didn't like the intensity. It was making everything feel weird.

"I need a drink. Want one?" I said, picking up my bag, knowing I needed to get out of there.

Dan shook his head. A small smile still remained on his face. I knew he was watching me as I left the room.

Later, at home, as I ran a shower, I glanced at my phone. Will had texted three times. A ripple of excitement passed through me. I couldn't believe he hadn't gone off me yet. I swept through the messages, trying to bite back the cheesy grin that was forcing its way out.

Baby . . . miss you. Bored. What you doing??

And:

Did I tell you how amazing your eyes are? Well, they are. . .

And:

Anna, Anna, Anna . . . I can't get you out of my head.

Three texts. It had to be a good sign, right? I'd hardly had anyone to judge it against; my experience with boys was pretty non-existent, unless you could count a quick snog with Alfie back in primary school (which lasted approximately two seconds). Now Will had come along and blown my mind.

I left the phone on my bed and jumped into the shower. I ached all over. I was sure it was the stress of living in this poxy tower and having to climb those stupid steps. Every day I cursed the fact we were here. I hated the flat. I hated the smell, the damp patches and the sour-faced neighbours.

I didn't even think much of my school. It hadn't been easy to make friends. It's not like I could ignore the evil looks and whispered comments – you'd think I'd come from Mars, not an estate across town. It was like most of the guys there seemed to think they'd got me all worked out. Estate girl, so I must be arrogant, maybe part of a gang. I must have a past, something to hide.

The truth was so dull it bored even me. The reality of being so poor that we used to hide from the bailiffs. The fact of having to buy clothes from charity shops and borrow money from Nan to pay for Christmas. The fact that my mum couldn't face living there any longer and ran off with Dad's best mate. The fact that Dad had sent me to a school halfway across the town in the deluded belief that it would keep me away from trouble. Away from the Mac. Yeah, great...

At least I'd found the band. Dan's music was keeping me sane.

I tipped my head back and let the water glide over my face. I could've stayed in there all day, but no doubt Eddie would be hammering on the door demanding a pee any second. My head was buzzing with thoughts, mainly Will of course. I could see his face so clearly behind my closed eyes – square jaw, cool, calm stare, his beautiful, wide smile. That cute little dimple just above the corner of his mouth. I could trace it with my finger. It was only there when he smiled and it was like he only seemed to smile for me.

In the other room, I could hear Eddie and Dad laughing as they played on the Xbox. They would be on it all evening. It was so noisy, it drove me insane. My dad's laugh was loud and booming, like a foghorn. He didn't laugh often these days – but when he did, it was always with Eddie.

I climbed out of the shower and wrapped a towel around me. I had homework to do but it was difficult to concentrate when my thoughts kept creeping back to Will. He was like an elastic band, pulling me towards him. I felt so psyched knowing I'd be seeing him again tomorrow. I had rehearsals again, but I had to see him first. I needed to.

I couldn't even bring myself to start my history work. Staring at the pages was sending me into a state of boredom. The words started to blur. I traced around the capitals. Reread the first sentence, wondering why nothing was sinking in.

Then my phone bleeped softly beside me.

I glanced down and saw Will had uploaded another picture. I opened it, biting my lip. It was him, just him. He looked so sad again, moody, his eyes drawn away from the camera. He had pulled up his top and I could see the soft lines of his chest.

I could have stared at it for ever.

He looked beautiful, like a film star.

My star.

Yeah, guess what? Mum's back in the land of living. Whoop-dee-bloody-do!

I'm due to see that stupid counsellor again tomorrow. What do I tell her? Hey, Mum's dancing round the living room to weird eighties music and chatting about us going on holiday. Is she for real? Most days she freaks out over leaving the house and now she's nattering on about plane tickets to Greece. She's sadly deluded, man...

Even her dancing is weird – all arms and bendy bodies, and then she starts singing in a high-pitched voice. Does she seriously think it's good? No one else does this freaky stuff, do they? Was it as bad when you were home? I don't think so. I know she could be difficult, but I swear she wasn't this – well – loopy.

I stand there watching her, confused and cringing at the same time. I can never bring people back here. How could I show this to Anna? "Hey, Anna, meet my mum. Don't mind the mad hair and the starey eyes. She just gets like this sometimes."

I don't fancy my chances of her sticking around. Anna's way too cool for any of this.

I guess Mum's not taking the meds again. Sometimes

she pours them down the sink. She says she doesn't need them. I can hardly make her, can I? She doesn't listen, even when I shout.

I can't watch her for long. I just get wound up. I want to walk like you did.

Why couldn't you have taken me with you?

I don't know what's worse. Crazy Mum or Crying Mum.

Which would you pick?

"Fear is a difficult thing – an energy that can eat you up if you let it." Debs stared at me, her face creased slightly in concern.

"It comes out of nowhere," I told her. My hands were curling and uncurling on my lap. "I hate the way it jumps out and grabs me. Sometimes I just feel . . . I don't know – like I can't control it."

"When was the last time you felt really anxious?"

"This morning," I said, my words flat, falling heavily from my dry mouth. "Dad was shouting. Telling me to clean the bedrooms. But I was already late. I didn't want to be even later."

Debs nodded, her head tilted a little.

"It wasn't fair," I continued. "Eddie never has to tidy, never. Only me. It's not fair. I threw a few bits on the bed but it wasn't good enough for him. He told me I was lazy. Told me I was selfish."

"How did that make you feel?"

"Useless. Rubbish, I suppose. How could I be lazy? I got Eddie's breakfast, didn't I? I ironed his clothes for school. I do loads."

"What happened next?"

"I threw a cup across the room. I didn't mean to, it didn't break or anything. I just wanted to shut him up and everything was buzzing inside. I wanted him not to say those things."

"I get that. I really do," she said.

"He said sorry then . . . I guess he felt bad. But that's not the point, is it?"

Debs was still nodding, her lips not moving but her eyes blazing into me.

"It's not right. I'm not. . ." My words stutter. I fell back against the chair, feeling empty.

"You're not what?"

"I'm not Mum." *I'm not.* Rage burning again.

I hated Debs and her stupid words. I wanted to get out of there. I didn't say anything more until the bell went. She kept talking, soft and gentle, but I'd tuned out. I couldn't hear any more.

Then I left silently, leaving the door wide open.

Will was waiting for me, leaning against the school

gate. I didn't like him seeing me after counselling, but once he found out, he'd insisted on meeting me. I always felt a bit jumbled afterwards, like I'd just been shaken up. It usually took a little while to get myself straight again. But at least Will knew what it was like.

"Yeah, they tried that stuff on me," he'd shrugged when I told him. "It's just all talk, talk, talk. Ticking their stupid boxes."

This time, he pulled me in for a kiss straight away, untucking my hair from behind my ears. "All right?" His eyes seemed to be wide with concern.

"I guess."

"You're making them happy by going, I suppose." He took my hand in his. His skin was always warm, yet not clammy. He squeezed tight. I was safe.

"Maybe I won't go again," I said. "It's a waste of time. I don't want to keep going over stuff."

"Well, you know what I said."

Will didn't seem to trust doctors, counsellors or teachers. In fact I didn't think he trusted many people. He said it was people like that who screwed things up for him in the past. I didn't want to ask any more, even though part of me longed to. I had a feeling it was to do with his mum. There had been whispers at school that she was a bit strange. Had

had some kind of a breakdown. I figured Will would tell me when he was ready. It was better to be a chilled girlfriend than a stressy, questioning one.

I felt sorry for him. Fancy having to deal with that. He seemed to cope so well. Was so strong.

Will said most teachers were idiots, trapped in their own little worlds. I didn't believe him at first, but I was starting to. I had never wanted to see a counsellor, but they had kept on at me. Why couldn't they see I was just fine as I was?

We started walking, hands locked. Will wasn't talking but I knew his brain was whirring. I knew he thought I should have missed the appointment completely. Maybe he was right. I wasn't sure any more; my head was churning.

"You've always got me to talk to," he said, squeezing my hand again.

I nodded – my way of saying thank you. It was nice of him. It made me feel shaky again, like I could cry. I blinked hard.

"I mean, is stuff really so bad that you need to talk to a stranger?"

"I guess not," I said, feeling my stomach lurch a little. "I just think people were worried about me."

"Why? Why do you need it?" he said, and then

stopped in his tracks. "Jeez, sorry, Anna. Just tell me to mind my own business. We've only been together for a short time and I'm already vetting you. I'm sorry. It's out of order."

"It's OK." I smiled, stroking the skin on the back of his hand. "Honestly. It's lovely of you to worry."

"No." He shook his head. "It's not. I should know better than that."

We started walking again. I could tell Will was upset. I hated seeing the frown on his face, didn't want him thinking he'd done something wrong. My skin was prickling; I wanted to make things better again. "Honestly, it's really nothing," I said. "I just get upset at school. Since Mum left, I find it difficult at home sometimes."

"She left?" His frown deepened. "When?"

"Six months ago. She found a new bloke and walked out. Moved to Brighton. We're meant to be visiting her soon, but . . . I don't know . . . I'm not ready yet, I guess. I don't even want to talk to her. She calls up, but I refuse to speak to her. I can't – not yet. . ."

"I'm sorry," he said. "That's harsh."

"I just miss her," I said, trying to fight back the tears again. "I miss her being at home. And now I have Dad stressing all the time. He seems angry at me for what happened, like it's my fault or something, like I made her go. On top of that my brother's a complete idiot."

Will stroked my hand with his thumb. "Sounds hard. It's like that for me sometimes . . . at home. . ."

"Really?"

"Yeah, it's not easy. My mum, she struggles. . ." Will's voice trailed off. "Listen, babe, it sounds to me that you just need to sound off now and again. I'd rather you do that with me. I think I get it. I know what it's like. Not some posh woman with a notepad and a file on how to talk to teenagers."

I nodded. "Yeah, I guess you're right."

We turned the corner, walked down the main high street. It was still quite busy. People pushed past us, bags looped through their arms, frowns creased deeply into their faces. Everyone looked so miserable, they always did.

"You don't need to worry about anything, Anna," he said. "Everything is going to work out perfectly."

I looked up at his sweet, serious face and thought – *yeah, you're right.*

Everything's going to be fine now.

"Why can't you pick anything up?"

I grabbed the socks that Eddie had left in a puddle on the floor. A glass was lying on its side, probably kicked over by his skanky feet.

Eddie just grunted, on his stomach on the sofa, watching some stupid rap programme on TV.

"Dad won't want you watching that."

"He doesn't mind."

I stood there glaring at him. At his long, skinny body. At his black, wild hair, much bushier than mine.

"Don't you need a shower or something?" I said.

"I don't want one."

"Seriously. When was the last time you washed? It's disgusting."

"Leave me alone," he muttered, his eyes still glued to the TV.

"You're rank."

I marched into the kitchen. Dad had left a note stuck to the fridge. He was obviously working a late shift that night.

Pizza in the fridge.
Make sure you wash up.
X

I looked at the one pathetic kiss, scrawled in a hurry, and wanted to scream. When was the last time he'd even hugged me? I pulled the note away and screwed it into a tight ball.

"I'm hungry," Eddie yelled.

"Yeah. Yeah – OK."

Dad's message went into the bin, on top of last night's potato peelings and his dirty cigarette ends.

Later, on my bed, I was using my laptop to talk to Will. So silly, but I hated the computer being between us. I wanted to reach out and touch him. Stroke his skin. Kiss those gorgeous lips again. Break through the screen and be with him.

"I don't want to be here," I said.

"Then come and meet me." His eyes twinkled. "Go on."

"I can't. Dad's not home yet."

Will sighed. "I really want to see you."

"It was only a few hours ago. . ."

He pulled a face. "I can't help it, can I? You're doing my head in."

"I don't want to be here though. I do want to be with you. I do."

He smiled. That smile. Such a killer.

"My life is so crap now," I muttered.

"No it's not!" He looked wounded.

"Not you, but here – home. It's all wrong. I actually think we hate each other. Well, they hate me anyway. Maybe I hate them too?"

"I'm sure you don't."

"What if it was Mum holding us together though. Now she's gone, maybe there's nothing keeping us together."

He shook his head at me. "Don't think that."

I sighed. "I'm tired. I'm probably not even making sense."

"You're looking dead cute though."

I rolled my eyes. "Will. . .!"

"Well! You are!"

"What you are doing, anyway?" I asked, wanting to change the subject. "What was your evening like?"

He sat back a bit, like he was really thinking about the question, a tiny crease – a pencil mark – denting his forehead. "Not much. Dinner. TV. That's it really."

"With your mum?"

His eyes flicked away from the screen and then back at me. They seemed sadder somehow. "Yeah, she was there."

Silence then. That was unusual. I picked at the stitches of my duvet and watched as he sat there, chewing on his lip.

"When can I see you?" he said finally.

"Tomorrow, at school."

"But when?"

I went through the timetable in my head. It was Friday, a busy day. "I meet the band at lunch tomorrow. It'll have to be after school, I guess. . ." I thought of Izzy and cringed – I was meant to be seeing her. I hoped she'd understand.

"Aw, seriously? I'm going to go crazy thinking about you."

"I'm sorry."

"How long do you have after school?"

"Not long. I have to get back to do dinner. I think Dad is on a late."

He groaned. "We need a plan. I have to see you more."

"I told you I hate my life," I muttered.

He reached forward and touched the screen, just one finger. "Don't hate it," he said. "We'll sort something soon."

"I'm sorry," I said.

"Don't be."

His eyes were twinkling back at me once more.

Inside I was swirling, hardly able to hide my excitement. It was like an addiction.

I just wanted to be with him again.

Hey, how's it going where you are? Been thinking of us at all? Have you?

Ha! That's doubtful...

Mum has pictures everywhere in the house. She talks to them. Talks to the faces like they're still here. On bad days she shouts at them. Today I caught her telling you how much she missed you and asking when you'd come back, like your stupid picture would answer.

I think she wishes she could take it all back.

Silly cow.

Do you know how many photos she has of me? One! One lousy picture, where I look young and stupid. And of course you're in it too!

Jeez, that stupid counsellor woman bangs on about anger and negative feelings. She should just spend ten minutes in our house, it's enough to send Mr Happy deranged. She's pleased I'm writing this stuff down though. I don't know why I'm doing it. Maybe it's because I want to prove her wrong. Or maybe it's because there's no one else to say this stuff to. I mean, let's face it, Mum has pretty much screwed up on that side of things. Could I seriously sit her down and have a conversation? One day she's likely to burst into tears, and the next, fly into a rage and blame me for everything.

Yeah, like it was my fault.

I could talk to Anna. I could. She is pretty amazing. But you know what? I don't want to. I don't want YOU to spoil that for me. If she knows all of this, you'll have your claws in that too. You'll wreck something else.

I set you alight after writing this. I enjoy that bit the most – watching the paper curl and blacken. Seeing my words turn to dust. I like the noise, the smell.

I think about that night a lot. What happened? Surely it couldn't have been that bad? Why couldn't you have stuck it out?

I have to.

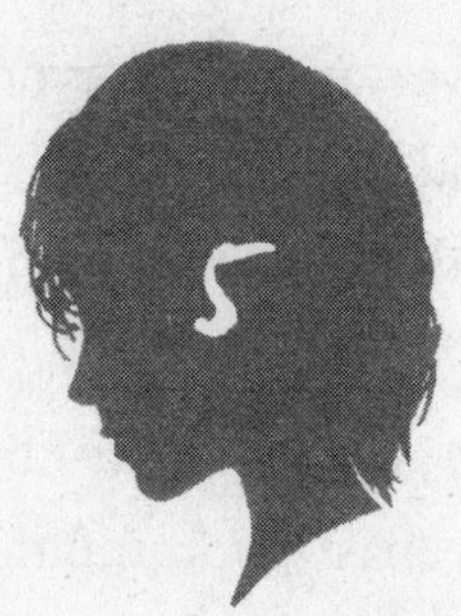

It had only been a few weeks and I could already see a change in Izzy. Will had warned me about it. Told me that mates can "get funny" when you get a boyfriend. *Don't ask me why, it's just some crazy girl thing. You can never be happy for each other.* He'd pulled a face as he'd said it, like he'd just eaten something disgusting. I got the feeling that he'd seen this happen lots of times before.

Even so, I hadn't believed him at first because Izzy had always been the most fab person ever. Totally cool. I guess I got that completely wrong.

Today she met me at the school gates as usual, but she had a face on her. It was a face that my mum used to say could sour milk. Just thinking of Mum made everything hurt inside. I wasn't sure I wanted to face Izzy's rage.

"You OK?" I asked.

She looked over at me. Her normally soft face seemed brittle and cold, like a mask. For a moment I wondered if I'd done something really serious, like slagged her off to someone and completely forgotten about it, but I quickly checked myself. I'd never, ever made nasty comments about her. Not even when I was really mad.

"What happened after school?" she asked. Her voice was quiet but icy.

"What? Yesterday?" My brain was whirring, trying to think. Where had I been? Then I remembered. "I was with Will. We went into town."

"Yeah, I know that. I saw you."

"You—" The words fell away. I realized that I was meant to have seen Izzy – to make up for all the times I'd rearranged plans. Crap. How did I forget that?

"I was hoping you'd help me get something for Nan," she said. "You know how important it is."

I went cold all over. Izzy's nan had been in a nursing home for a few months now and was getting really frail. It was her birthday and Izzy wanted to buy her something special, and she'd wanted my input.

"I'm sorry," I said. "We can go today if you want."

Except today I was meant to be seeing Will

again. I couldn't see him at lunch, so that was my only time. I felt torn. I didn't want to upset either of them.

"Don't worry yourself," Izzy snapped. "I sorted it."

"I really am sorry. I forgot."

Izzy pulled at the strap of her backpack. Her eyes darted away from me. "Every lunch you're either in rehearsals or with Will. I never see you after school any more. You don't answer texts." She sighed. "It's a bit rubbish."

"I'll sort something. I'll talk to Will. Maybe we can do something, just us two?" I said.

"I'm not asking much, Anna. But I never thought we'd let *some guy* get between us."

The "some guy" comment rang out. I paused for a second, wondering why that stung so much. I could imagine Will standing there, shaking his head. *What did I tell you? She's jealous.*

"But he's not some guy, is he? I really like him." I paused. "I'm sorry if I've been pushing you out though."

Izzy shrugged; she didn't seem that bothered. Maybe I was being oversensitive. "It's OK," she said. "I was just saying. It's no big deal really."

"So how about I sort something? Maybe a cinema trip this Friday?"

Izzy grinned. "That'll be cool. And Will won't mind?"

"No, of course he won't."

I saw Will sooner than I expected to. He turned up at the end of rehearsals that lunchtime. Dan elbowed me and gestured towards the door.

"I think you have an admirer."

I looked up and saw him leaning against the door frame. He looked bored and was playing with his phone, not even looking at me.

"When did he get here?" I hissed at Dan.

"Only a few minutes ago," he said, grinning. "Why? You trying to keep him hidden away?"

It wasn't that at all and Dan knew it. I hated anyone watching me sing. It freaked me out. It was different being onstage, more detached somehow. And I was fine singing to the rest of the band; they were used to me, they were like my family. But singing raw, in front of someone else, was gut-wrenchingly unbearable. I hated the thought. Even worse, our current song was a duet. Less dark than usual and more intense. Dan liked us to look at each other and that freaked me out even more.

"I'd better go," I said.

"So soon," Dan said, his grin stretching. "Don't you want to go over the chorus again? We're in such good harmony today."

I smacked him on the arm. "Don't start!"

"I love it when you flirt with me," Dan teased back.

"I love it when you shut your trap." Despite myself I was smiling. "Same time tomorrow?"

Dan nodded, his eyes flicking over towards Will. "I think lover boy is getting restless."

Will was looking straight at Dan. His phone was away now. His face was still and unreadable. Then he saw me looking and his lazy smile returned.

"Hey, babe," he said, strolling over. "I couldn't wait till later so I thought I'd pop by. Say hello."

"Did you hear much?" I asked, panicking a bit. I swear I was so out of tune. He must've thought I was the worst singer ever. The thought of it made me feel sick.

He frowned and then said, "No. No, I've only just arrived."

"Cool." I grabbed his hand. "Come and meet the others. I want you to love them as much as I do."

Max was still at his drum kit, on his phone. He waved at Will. Chris was sitting with Dan at the back of the room. I led him over. Dan looked up straight away.

"Hey, mate. I'm Dan. I remember you from primary school."

Will stared at him blankly, "Erm. No not really. But it was a long time ago. Good to meet you though."

"You heard our stuff before?" Chris asked. He was probably the quietest out of the four of us, but he took the band really seriously. And he was an excellent bassist.

"I saw you in concert. It was OK," Will said.

"Just OK?" Dan asked, a small smile curling.

"Just OK," Will said. "Bit dark, if I'm honest."

The two guys stared at each other for a bit. Will casually looked Dan up and down. His eyes were dead cold.

"Well – good to meet you, mate," Dan said finally. He shot me a look before turning away.

Will took my hand. "Let's get out of here."

As we marched out of the room, I could feel myself prickle with anger. "What was all that about?"

"What?"

"You! With him. You were really moody. He noticed, you know."

"Good," Will muttered.

"What?" I pulled away from him. "What do you mean good? These are my mates – I really care about them."

"And I'm your boyfriend."

"So?"

"So. . ." He sighed. "Look. I've got my reasons. I don't like Dan. I've heard stuff about him."

"Like what?"

He paused, then shook his head. I could see his cheeks were reddening. He looked really upset. "No, it's not fair. I'm listening to gossip. I shouldn't do that. It's out of order."

"What gossip?"

"Babe," he said, stroking my face. "It really doesn't matter. I'll make more effort next time."

I was softening. "Promise?"

"Promise."

We walked out of school together. It was getting chilly. I pulled my cardigan tight against me and sucked in the sharp evening air.

"You know, I'm so lucky to have met you."

Will squinted back at me. "Really? You think so?"

"Yeah, of course. Apart from Izzy. Apart from the band – no one else talks to me. I'm the boring, quiet one. I'm not sure I've ever fitted in here. Not really."

Will squeezed my hand. "You're so far from boring."

"Thank you."

"And you're in a band. Doesn't that make you really cool anyway?"

"Not me personally. But it is cool being part of something like that," I said. "And it's cool being with you."

Will rocked back a bit; his expression was chilled, but I think he was secretly pleased. Then slowly he reached forward and unclipped my hair. I squealed in shock. "Ugh. I look a right mess now!"

"You look gorgeous this way." His hands fanned my hair out around my face, gently stroking my skin as he did so. "I told you before; you should always have it like this."

"I can't in school. I'll look like a total tramp."

"Screw school. You'll look just fine."

I paused. "Do you like school?" I asked.

Will didn't answer for a minute. He stared

straight out across the road in front of where we were sitting. Finally he sighed. "It's OK, I guess. I just get irritated sometimes. Everyone seems so lame, worried about the next party or getting drunk. I guess I have bigger plans."

I smiled. "Like what?"

He turned to me. "Like getting away. Don't you dream about that?"

I thought about Dad, the arguments. I thought about my singing, how good that made me feel. How I had a secret ambition to leave this stupid town and become a new person – a more confident me. Lit up on a stage somewhere, just me and my music.

"I guess – sometimes," I said, softly.

"I'll do my exams. Then I'm getting a place of my own. It'll be perfect, just how I want it."

"Away from here?"

Will turned to me; his eyes seemed to soften. "Who knows?"

I slowed up and thought about this. I kept forgetting Will was older. He could go to college soon if he wanted. Was there a chance he wouldn't be around any more?

"I'd still need to see you though," he said softly, like he was reading my mind.

Flutters in my tummy, like flower petals in the breeze. "Really?"

"Really . . . I know it's only been a short time, but you're so, so special."

He leant towards me and his lips were on mine, gentle at first, like a breath. Then firmer and intense, hot, drawing me towards him.

In that moment, all I could see was us.

I tried telling Mum about Anna today. The conversation went like this:

Me: Mum, I've met this girl.

Her: Hmmm. There's nothing for tea. Can you phone in a pizza?

Me: Sure, that's fine, but I met this girl, Mum. She's amazing.

Her: Hmmm. A girl . . . Oh, nice.

Me: Yeah. She's called Anna. She's pretty and smart.

Her: A man knocked today. I didn't know who he was so I didn't let him in. He said he was from the council. But you never know, do you? He's back tomorrow, so I guess whatever it is can wait...

Me: I guess so. But did you hear me, Mum?

Her: Maybe you could call them for me. Tell them I'm not well or something?

Me: OK.

Her: What were you saying before?

Me: About Anna?

Her: No. About ringing for a pizza?

See. It's useless. A joke. Even when I want her to know stuff, even when I try and let her in – she ruins it. Every bloody time.

I don't want to end up nutty like her.

"I still don't know why he had to come?" Izzy hissed at me.

"He really wanted to see the film. I don't see the problem," I said. "Anyway. It gives you a chance to get to know him better."

Will was at the ticket office, paying for us. I felt bad for him. I didn't want him picking up on Izzy's negative vibes. It had been so nice of him to offer to get our tickets. He'd been so keen to come when I'd mentioned it, how could I have said no?

"I thought this was time for us." Izzy's face was dark, unmoving.

"Yeah, it is. I thought this was a way I could hang out with both of you. Will wants to get to know you. He thought it would be a good opportunity."

Izzy turned a little, started fiddling on her phone. It was clear she was stressed. I decided to ignore her and focused instead on Will. He was chatting with the guy at the counter. I could see him smiling, probably making a joke. Inside I was raging a little. I really didn't see what the big deal was. I'd never known Izzy to be like this before.

"Maybe I should go? Leave you two to it?" Izzy said.

"Don't be so daft. That's not what we want."

"What *we* want?"

"What I want, then!"

Izzy continued to glare, but she didn't move. A small shrug told me she was staying. I'd never seen her like this before. I wondered if she was jealous. It was no secret that she wanted a boyfriend. Will told me girls get like that sometimes.

Will marched back over, grinning. "Shall we get some popcorn, then?"

"I'm not fussed," Izzy muttered.

"I'd love some," I said, smiling back.

We walked over to the refreshments. Will hung back a little and started to speak to Izzy. "Anna talks about you so much, it's great to meet you properly."

"She does?" Izzy seemed surprised.

"Yeah, of course."

"Well, she talks about you all the time," she said

sweetly. Too sweetly. Will grinned but I didn't like the way she said it. Her eyes were still cold.

"I've seen you at school. Aren't you in the basketball team or something?"

"Yeah, I am," Izzy said. "I'm surprised you'd know that. I didn't think girls' sport would be your thing."

Will seemed to consider this for a second, frowned slightly and then shook his head. "Nah. Not my thing. I guess I just saw you guys training or something."

I glared at Izzy, hating her for giving Will such a hard time. Couldn't she just relax? Be happy for me? My eyes kept darting towards him. Couldn't Izzy see what a big deal this was for me? This was Will Bennett, not some geeky Year Nine kid.

"Popcorn, then?" Will said. He smiled at me. He seemed to be telling me it was all still OK.

As he left to get me some, Izzy turned to me again. "How come he knows I'm on the basketball team?"

"I don't know. What's so strange about that – it's hardly a secret."

Izzy sighed. "I don't know." She shook her head, curls bouncing. "It's probably just me. I'm sorry."

My stomach twisted. "No, what is it? What are you saying?"

"I don't know, Anna. Maybe I'm being protective of you. I just worry that—"

Will walked back to us then, two overflowing tubs in his hands. "Are you sure I couldn't get you any, Izzy?" he said. "It looks so good. I feel awful leaving you out."

"I'm fine, really."

"You can always have mine, if you change your mind," he said, his smile wide.

"Thanks." She turned her head slightly, looking out towards the crowd. It was a tiny gesture, but I noticed it. Why couldn't she be nice to him?

"C'mon, then," he motioned towards the doors.

I hung back deliberately, catching Izzy as she moved away. "He's great, Izzy, you just don't know him yet. Try. For me, please."

Izzy looked at me, big wide eyes, and then nodded weakly. "Of course," she said.

We caught up with Will, who was already waiting by the door. He looked puzzled, worried maybe. I stroked his arm.

Inside the dark room, he stood back to let me lead. I found us some seats near the back and was forced to shuffle into place. It wasn't until I sat down that I realized that Izzy wasn't next to me.

Will was sitting between us.

Will insisted on coming back on the bus with me.

"It's late. I don't want you going to that estate on your own."

"What about Izzy?" She was standing a little away from us, texting again. She'd been quiet since the film and was now standing with her coat clutched tightly around her.

"Izzy will be OK," he said, turning towards her. "Hey, Iz. How are you getting home?"

"My dad's picking me up," she said. "He can take you home too, Anna. If you want?"

"Nah. It's OK, I'm taking her," Will said.

"Really?" Izzy's eyes were bright. "Bit out of your way? My dad is driving; it'll take half the time."

"I want to," Will said coolly.

She looked at me and I smiled back. "I think I'll go with Will," I said.

She nodded, but her face couldn't hide the scowl. "Fine. You better hurry, then. Don't want to miss the last bus."

"I don't want to just leave you," I said, suddenly

aware of her isolation, of the crowds of people around us, jostling and shouting. She seemed smaller somehow, more vulnerable.

"She said she'd be fine," Will said, tugging on my arm. He nodded towards Izzy, made a sort of grunting noise that I guessed was a "bye, good to meet you". Izzy managed a tight grin, but it seemed fake – not anything I'd seen from her before.

Before I could say anything more, Will took my hand and led me across the road, past the dwindling crowds and bright lights of the complex. I quickly looked back, but I'd already lost Izzy amongst the churning mists of people.

"Jeez, that was hard work," he breathed.

"She's not normally like that," I said. "I hope she'll be OK."

The evening air was cool, a light drizzle dancing in the breeze, barely touching our skin. We moved fast, coats whipping and feet slapping the pavement in time.

"She doesn't like me," Will said.

"She just didn't like the set-up. It was meant to be a girls' night," I sighed. "It was my fault."

"I thought she'd like to meet me. What's her problem? I swear she must be jealous of you."

My head was buzzing. "You think?"

"Yeah, of course. Why else would she get a strop on like that? Look at you. So beautiful. Clever and funny and now. . ." His words hung between us.

"And now I'm dating you," I teased. "The sex god."

"No! No, that's not what I meant. But now we're together and she doesn't like it."

"I guess she was a little strange tonight."

"Trust me. I know what I'm talking about."

I didn't want to push him on what he meant, but I did feel completely confused by the whole thing. What sort of friend was Izzy if she couldn't relax and enjoy an evening with me and my boyfriend? I'd do that for her. Wouldn't I? She'd made the whole thing so strange and awkward.

We reached the bus stop just in time. Will dropped my hand. "See! I said we had to be quick!"

"You don't have to ride with me," I said. "My flat is right by a stop. I haven't got to walk far."

"It's no problem."

We got on quickly. The bus was quiet. I saw some guys sat towards the back, hunched up together – dark clothing and hoods draped over their faces. At the front sat an older woman, dressed in beige and completely stiff. She was clutching her handbag and casting the boys suspicious looks – every inch of her suggested she was both disgusted and afraid. I wanted to tell her to loosen up, but my small smile as we passed was quickly met with an upturned snarl. She shrank back from me, like I was dirty or something. I felt myself tense. It was like I could read her mind. I knew exactly what she was thinking. She saw me as another kid from the estates. A waste of time.

Don't judge me. Don't you dare...

We found a seat at the back. Will pressed me up against the dark, smoky glass. On the metallic sheeting below there was graffiti – dark hearts and unreadable tags. I kept staring at the old woman's back, wondering what had happened to make her so angry. Why was I letting it stress me out so much?

Will seemed to notice my mood. "You OK?" he said.

"Mmm, just tired..."

"Hey – you look so amazing," he said. "Can I take a photo?"

I hate my picture being taken, but I didn't want to say no to him. I nodded mutely. He raised his phone, grinning, and started pressing the button. Then he showed me. I wasn't sure how many he'd actually taken. Most had been serious, but on the last I had stuck my tongue out.

"I like that one the best," he said, saving it as his screensaver. "You look full of life."

I smiled, but inside I felt twisted and hot. I was still raging at the stupid old woman and her attitude towards me. But I was also angry at Izzy.

Why couldn't she get along with Will? Or at least try for my sake.

The estate never looked particularly welcoming at the best of times. But by late evening, it was beyond grim. There was something about the impending dark, the slow drop in temperature and the gang that was starting to collect at the foot of the towers, that made it more oppressive, more foreboding. Most of the gang just skated about or smoked or whatever, but sometimes they gave you grief – it depended what mood they were in.

I was used to it. Will wasn't.

He looked up at the huge twin blocks and scowled. "Nice," he said, his voice dripping with sarcasm.

"I guess you live in a posh place," I bit back. I couldn't help myself.

Will said nothing, he just kept staring up at the towers like they were some well-known place. In the end I had to drag him down the narrow walkway that led to Tower A. "You must hate it here," he said.

"I'm used to it."

"You seriously don't belong here."

"It's fine, honestly."

I saw some of the lads look over at us. One shouted something, but I couldn't make it out. They all laughed. They probably knew Will wasn't from round here, don't ask me how, maybe he was giving off some vibe or something. Maybe it was the way he moved. Thank god he didn't have his school uniform on. I got enough hassle for going to a "posh school", but a kid who lived out of the area wouldn't be so easily forgiven. Posh kids were generally sneered at – they didn't understand us.

As we came towards the entry door, it sprang open and Lyn came out. I knew him from around the estate. Most people do; he's kind of important like that. He was OK. One of the better ones. Most days he was friendly and not too full of himself.

"All right?" he said, nodding at me.

"Yeah," I said back.

Lyn cast a quick, scathing glance in Will's direction and then set off across the walkway.

"Who's that?" Will asked, turning to follow his departing body.

"Who? Lyn? Just a lad from here. I barely know him."

"Oh." He shot him one final look and then turned back to me. "OK."

I was at the door now, but there was no way I could let Will come inside with me. Not with Dad home anyway. "Thanks for walking me back," I said.

"No worries. I like keeping you safe."

He leant forward and held my shoulders, pulling me towards him. I was aware of other kids probably watching us, but Will didn't seem to care. He tugged me forward with quite a bit of force and kissed me firmly on the lips.

"Wow," I said. "You're not messing around."

"I've been waiting all night to do it."

He kissed me again, a bit softer now, but still gripping my shoulders. I could feel each finger pressing into me. It was just beginning to get a little uncomfortable before he released me. I could feel the blood pumping under my skin.

"But I still say you don't belong here. No way," he said.

"But I. . ."

"No. You deserve better."

I got in late tonight. After seeing Anna, I walked home. I like walking. It gives me space to think stuff through.

The Mac Estate is pretty dire though. It's just a cesspit. A pit full of losers.

I came home over the wall, straight through the back door. Mum was talking to herself in the living room – having a full-on conversation with the invisible man. She must find him more interesting than me, I guess.

She'll be back in bed soon. More days crying and blaming the world for everything. More days of me watching her not eat, not interact, not go out. More days wondering how long this can go on before someone explodes.

I can do better than this.

OK, I wasn't stupid, I knew Izzy was really annoyed with me. Days had gone by without her replying to my texts and, to be honest, I was sick of being blanked in lessons. Although we still sat together, she would have her stuff out first and be busy writing when I arrived. Or she'd be laughing with the other girls, making sure not to include me. She barely said a word to me. When I mentioned the cinema, she just flapped her hand and said, "Don't worry about it."

"We'll do something else," I said.

"Whatever. It's not a big deal. I know you're busy."

I could hear the ice in the word "busy", but I chose to ignore it. I couldn't let myself get stressed. Will said girls get like that, he'd seen it before. I just hoped she'd chill out pretty soon.

What got me through school were Will's texts. When we weren't walking to lessons together, we were sending messages. I was getting good at hiding my phone under my book, or between the flaps of my skirt. Will would text me constantly – asking how I was, who I was sitting with. It was sweet, reassuring. It thrilled me just how many messages he could send in a day. I'd heard the other girls moaning, saying their guys barely acknowledged them in school, and I glowed with a kind of smugness.

Will wasn't like that.

One time, as I sat in a boring history lesson, letting my brain turn to mush, I felt my phone vibrate under my hand.

> You've put your hair up. Wear it down. You know I like it better like that.

I looked around – stupidly. How did he know? I'd only pulled it back minutes before. I still found it hard having my hair loose all the time; it annoyed me. My eyes flicked over to the glass door, but there was no one there. I quickly texted back, my hair now released, which helped to disguise my actions.

How did you know?

It didn't take long for the answer to appear.

I sneaked out of lesson. I just wanted to see you – even for a second.

I beamed. Jeez, he was so cute. I ran my hands through my free strands, reminding myself how much he loved it like that.

Will walked me to rehearsals, our hands locked together. I was using the time I'd usually grab something to eat to see him. Now Izzy was blanking me there was little point of going to the canteen anyway. Will didn't like being there. He said it was where the "idiots" hung about. My stomach was growling though. I'd missed breakfast that morning.

"How's it going anyway?" Will asked. "You never talk about your music stuff."

"It's good. There's not much to say really."

I was beginning to feel a bit sick; my stomach felt like it was full of air. I stopped by the water fountain so that I could open my bag. I always had emergency rations there, usually to eat on the bus on the way home.

"I'd love to know more about it. It seems so important to you and I want to understand it more."

I was searching through my bag, distracted. "What's to understand? I sing, probably not that well. Dan's good though – really good." I looked up. "He's the one with the talent."

Will was picking at the paint on the wall. "Is he?"

"God yeah, he writes the most amazing music and the lyrics are just to die for. I swear I never liked that sort of music before – but when I first heard them play I was hypnotized or something. Dan thinks they work better with a female lead, but his voice is just as good."

"He sounds pretty impressive." Will was still picking. He'd made a small crater in the wall, flower-shaped.

"He is. I really think he could make it and— aw, there it is!" I pulled out a chocolate bar.

"Is that all you're eating?" Will frowned as I unwrapped it. The little crease between his eyes deepened – it always did this when he was worried, or stressed.

"I won't get a chance to have anything else. It's fine." I started eating. It tasted warm and sweet. My stomach seemed to settle instantly. "And remember I have counselling last period, so I might be late out of school."

He sighed. "Yeah, what a waste that is. . ."

"I'll just try one more. It seems fair." I swallowed the last bite, licking my fingers. It tasted so good.

"Anna, chocolate isn't good for you. You shouldn't binge like that."

"It's not a binge. It's one bar." I stuffed the wrapper in my bag. "C'mon, I'm going to be late for Dan."

We moved away again. "I just like you to be careful. That's all. I don't want you—"

"Want me what?" I looked up at him, confused.

"Oh – it doesn't matter." He gripped my hand again. "Like you said, we better get a move on."

We walked on quicker, but somehow the chocolate didn't taste so good in my mouth.

"So you don't like people judging you?" Debs said, softly. "Who does?"

"I don't know why it winds me up. I just hate the funny looks I get sometimes. Like this woman on the bus a few nights ago. They think they know me. They know nothing."

"Who does know you?"

I sank back further on the chair, cool material against my sweaty skin. My hand started tracing the swirling patterns on the wooden arm – round and round. "I don't know," I said finally. "Will, I guess. He seems to know me pretty well."

"That's good. You've not been together that long." She leant forward, eyes gleaming. "It must be going well for you to trust him so soon."

"Really well. He's good for me."

"How long has it been?"

"Just a few weeks. But it's special. You wouldn't get it."

Debs shook her head gently. "No, maybe I wouldn't. Relationships are private, beautiful things. Only you truly know how they're going."

I nod.

"But who else is there? Along with Will, who else really understands you?" Her voice was so soft, floating between us. I imagined her words in little bubbles, pricking against my skin.

"My mum – used to . . . I guess." My voice was breaking, failing me. I swallowed back the tears that wanted to come. "We used to talk sometimes, about all sorts of stuff. The future, our dreams, everything. She'd play me music and we'd sing together. She had such an amazing voice."

"Is that where you get it from – the voice?"

"I guess. But she was much better. Dad used to say she was, like, amazing. He used to cry just listening to her."

I shrink back further, thinking about the two of them. Dad's muscly arm around her tiny, trim waist. They would both laugh, Dad's voice booming over hers. They always seemed so happy.

"He must have loved her."

"He did. He really did. He did everything for her, but I guess it was never enough."

I think of the letters that Dad would stress over, the people at the door. Mum's flash car being taken away. We could never afford the life she wanted.

"Have you spoken to her? Since?"

"I don't want to." My words like bullets now, popping her stupid bubbles.

"Why?"

"Because we weren't good enough for her." The rage was pumping now, burning inside me.

"We were never enough. And that's why she went. I have nothing else to say to her."

"Do you think. . . ?"

My eyes were shut, arms folded. I had to push the bad stuff back.

"I have nothing to say," I said.

I didn't.

Not having a dad around is no big deal really. Not now. I guess I'm just used to it.

It's not like there's much of a gap there any more. I barely notice.

> *Q. Who is your dad?*
>
> *A. Some bloke who was around when I was a kid. He phones sometimes when he feels like it. Do I remember him? Not so much...*

But I hate it that I'm doing this alone.

It wasn't always like this. Mum was OK but right after you left, she fell apart, like completely lost it. The clothes you left behind, she tore up – it was majorly scary. I kept thinking you'd come back any day. Everything would be OK – you'd come home, Mum would calm down, everything would be normal. Or normal-ish.

Ha ha.

I got that totally wrong, then.

She's crying again now. I can still hear her. It's been loads of naff tears and soppy love songs. She grips her hands together like she's praying and listens to this wet, lame music until my ears ring. She says it helps her. She says it helps her forget.

She doesn't look like she's doing much forgetting from where I'm standing.

"So you can't meet me this lunch either?" Will said.

"No. I'm sorry. I've already arranged with Dan."

Will scowled and then nodded. "It's OK. I'll meet Zak and Callum. I keep ditching them. They've been moaning a bit."

I laughed. "So you don't mind?"

The morning sun was sparkling against the school building, almost blinding me. The bell was about to go any minute; we had seconds before the day started. I felt annoyed, wanted to freeze time. It seemed like I only had precious minutes with Will and they disappeared in an instant.

"Of course I don't mind. It's cool," he said, kissing me lightly on the head.

I watched as he walked away, his tall, lean body moving with confidence. I felt myself tingle all over, hardly able to believe this was still happening. Just weeks before I'd been alone, a nothing. Now I had so much. It was exciting, unreal.

I wanted to laugh out loud. Shout after him.

Hey, come back! Just stay with me!

But of course I didn't, I just watched. I watched as a group of his mates greeted him at the main doors. I watched as he threw his arm round one of them, Zak I think, and laughed.

I watched as he disappeared through the doors, out of sight.

Why was I so disappointed that he hadn't turned back?

Izzy was already there when I arrived in the form room. She looked towards me, then away, turning her chair to face Abbie and Faye behind us. I sat down and could feel the frost like it was coming out of her body in spiky icicles.

"All right?" I said.

"Oh yeah," Izzy replied, and Abbie sniggered.

My stomach burned. "Look," I said, leaning towards her. "I was thinking it might be nice if we met up later this week. What do you reckon? Shopping or something?"

"Nah, it's OK. I'm going with Abbie tonight."

Abbie grinned back at me, as if to reinforce the point. I wanted to slap her stupid face, but of course I didn't. I just sat there like a muppet, feeling like the most unwanted person in the room. "I understand, I know I've not been around much," I said softly.

I felt Izzy flinch next to me. "You could say that. . ."

"How's your nan anyway? I've not seen her in so long," I whispered.

Izzy turned back to face me; her eyes seemed to soften for a second. "She's . . . well, no different really. I might go there again tomorrow."

I nodded. "I hope it goes OK."

"You could always come? My nan would love to see you. She's always liked you." Izzy was really staring at me. I felt like I was being tested or something.

"I was meant to be seeing Will—"

"Oh, of course." Her words bit through mine. "I knew you'd say that. Look, don't bother."

"I was going to say I could ask him. I'll sure he'll understand."

Izzy shook her head softly. "You shouldn't have to ask, Anna."

I was about to say that that was what being in

a relationship was all about and she obviously had no clue, but Izzy had turned around again. It was hopeless. Pathetic. I couldn't face talking to her back, so I slouched in my chair. Izzy carried on chatting with the other two. I half listened to their stupid conversation about some party last weekend, knowing I wasn't included.

All around me, everyone was talking, laughing. The boys were crowded by the window, taking bets on whether a fight was going to break out between some Year Tens. I looked over at them and realized just how bored I was by it all, how restless I felt. I just wanted to walk out. Find Will and go somewhere. The Swamp, maybe. Sit under the trees again. Chill. Not listen to this . . . rubbish.

"So I'm guessing you don't want to meet for lunch?" Izzy said suddenly.

She was back facing me now. Calm, unfriendly expression. Mouth set in a firm line. Eyes cool. This was another test. I was sick of it. It wasn't my fault she was jealous.

"I have rehearsals," I said, flatly.

"So you're not seeing Will either?"

"Is that all this is about? Whether I'm seeing Will or not?"

"Maybe? It's pretty much like you're glued to him at the moment."

"I like being with him," I said. "He is my boyfriend. I'm meant to want to be with him."

"So if you didn't have rehearsals – you'd be with him?"

I shrugged. "I guess."

Izzy kept staring at me for like the longest time. Then she sat back, her eyes switching to the front of the room.

"You should never forget your mates," she said softly.

"I haven't," I hissed.

But the words were lost on her. It was clear we couldn't agree.

Dan threw the guitar to one side and groaned. He looked hot. His face was glowing red and his cheeks were puffed out in frustration. He swiped a hand over his face.

"Anna, we can't keep going over this. Why aren't you getting it?"

"I'm sorry," I spat back. "I guess I'm not in the right frame of mind just now."

It was so hot in that stuffy room. How was I

expected to concentrate on music when I was so sticky and uncomfortable? Everyone else would be stretched out in the sun, enjoying their lunch break, and what was I doing? Getting grief from Dan – who was obviously in one of his stress-head moods.

This, after my morning of coldness from Izzy. Not only that but Will hadn't texted me all day. It wasn't like him. I was used to his hundreds of messages. A picture, maybe. Sometimes he would even pop up outside my class and walk with me to the next lesson.

But today, nothing. Complete silence.

"We really need to sort this," Dan muttered. "It's not like you haven't had weeks to work on it."

"I've been busy."

"Yeah – so we've heard." Dan raised an eyebrow to the others. Chris stifled a laugh. I felt myself redden.

"What do you mean?"

Dan had his smug face on. "Nothing. I meant nothing."

"He's just winding you up," Chris said.

"Obviously," I said. "But I'd like to know what he's getting at."

"I just meant you've been a bit . . . well, occupied. Everyone's seen you two. You're like the new hot couple or something. Permanently glued to each other."

"So?"

"So. . . That's fine, if you like that sort of thing."

Chris sniggered again. I swear I was ready to punch him.

"Should I bother carrying on with this song or what?" I said, my voice rising.

Dan snorted. "You've just gotta chill a bit, Anna. It's not our fault your voice is all over the place."

I shook my head. I was seriously stressed now. The warmth in there was intensifying. I was getting so uncomfortable. I shuffled in my seat and thought about walking out – but I really wanted to get the tune bang on. But annoyingly, my voice seemed to be wobbly, almost straining against the words. I knew Dan had noticed I was struggling. He probably thought I wasn't as committed or something.

It didn't help that they kept shooting sarky remarks about me and Will.

Why the hell was everyone so interested in my love life anyway? I'm sure no one blinked when Dan dated half of Year Nine. Why was this suddenly a huge deal?

"I'm surprised people are interested in me," I muttered.

"Where Will's concerned – people are interested." Dan's eyes were gleaming. "Jeez, Anna, you can't date the school stud and not expect people to gossip."

Words were burning inside me, the need to scream *This is nothing to do with our music. With you. With anything.* Instead I sat back, took a deep breath and looked Dan straight in the eye. "Can we just get on with this, please?"

Dan laughed. "Ooooh, tetchy!"

"Don't push me!" I warned. "Honestly, I've just about had enough."

He seemed to consider me for a minute before shrugging and picking his guitar up. Without saying another word, he slowly started to strum. The room, already thick with heat, was now filled with music. I stood up, and before I could doubt myself, I blasted the words out.

"I can't stop this pain
Words are blows they tear my brain
Your love drives me insane
Nothing left for us to gain."

The sound was beautiful. My voice was rich. It seemed to dance right there in front of me and then carry across the room. The hairs on my arms prickled and tears stung my eyes. As the words flowed, my body was on fire. I felt taller somehow, like I was towering over all of them.

I was alive. I was in total control.

I stood for a second, the echoes of the song still dancing in my ears. I swear a new energy was racing through me, buzzing and stirring me. I shivered with emotion.

As I got up to leave, Dan touched my arm.

"I was only messing," he said. "I didn't mean to wind you up."

"Well, you did," I said, and walked away.

"It sounds as though music is important to you," Debs said.

We were coming to the end of our session and I'd just told her about the rush of excitement after nailing the song. It felt like I imagined flying did. Feeling that rush of air around you, knowing that you couldn't fall, knowing you were in complete control.

"It is." I picked at the clammy leather on her

chair, trying to remember that feeling, hold on to it. "I get so stressed when it goes wrong – but when it's right, it's like nothing else."

"Like a release?"

"I guess."

"Did you need a release today?"

My thoughts jumped back to Dad's angry face this morning, to Izzy's accusations, to Dan's barbed comments, to not seeing Will. I couldn't answer, but she saw something change in my face.

"You look exhausted," she said, softly.

"I'm fine."

"What was your morning like?"

"The usual. Got up. Got ready. Sorted Eddie out. Dad had a go at me – no difference really."

"Why did he have a go?" Her head dipped slightly. "You don't have to tell me if you don't want to. I'm just interested."

"I forgot to wash his trousers for work, that's all. He's really stressed at the moment, more than usual. He likes everything to be ready so that he can leave on time. I made him late by forgetting."

"Why do you think he's so stressed?"

I thought about this for a minute – did I honestly know? "Mum leaving, I guess. Maybe he doesn't like looking after us much. Saying that, he's OK with Eddie; he doesn't get so snappy with him." I paused, drew a long shaky breath. "I suppose his work is tough. He drives a cab and sometimes he gets hassle. He works long hours. I know he gets tired. It can't be easy. Me and Eddie don't get on either, we're always yelling at each other – he hates that."

"It must be hard on all of you."

I snorted. "Not on Eddie. He gets to do exactly what he likes now. Dad gives him such an easy ride."

Debs sat back, her hands carefully knitted together on her lap. I kept staring at her nails. So neat, so carefully painted. I hated my bitten, ripped-up ones; they made me feel stupid for some reason – like I couldn't take care of myself, or wasn't bothered. Will had made a comment once, looked at my fingers and frowned. *You should look after yourself, babe.* Thinking about that made me cringe.

"Do you think Eddie is happy though?" Debs said, softly. "Do you really think this is what your brother wants?"

I thought then of Eddie. Of him lazing on

our sofa. Of him flicking his finger up at me, his chocolate-smeared face leering up at me.

"Yeah," I said. "I think he's the only one who's got what he wants."

I hated him for it.

Things are developing. Yeah, things are moving along at speed. I can barely keep up.

For one thing – I've stopped counselling. That woman was driving me mad with her stupid ideas and soppy smile. I couldn't face it any more, so I jacked it in. I don't think she was too surprised. It wasn't like we had an amazing relationship or anything.

Second of all – Mum is taking her meds again. Obviously it'll take us a while to see the full effects, but at least she's out of bed. She sits in front of the TV now, mainly watching old films – weird ones that never made it to the cinema. They usually involve heavily made-up women searching for some slick-haired man to save the day. It's pretty creepy but she seems to like them.

At least the sobbing has stopped.

Third of all – Anna is great.

I'm not going to say too much, because I don't want to ruin it.

I'm chilled at the moment. I'm happy.

I'm in control now.

It was weird, having him there, in my flat.

I mean, yeah, it was cool. Dad was working. Eddie had been bribed with some cash. It was a perfect chance to be alone. Even so, I wasn't used to having a boy in my space, sitting on my bed, looking at my stuff. Even worse, I knew Eddie would be hovering outside, trying to nose, the sly little sneak.

Will wanted this. After being a bit cool with me, he called and asked to see me. Asked for "proper" time together. I was aching to see him after days of limited text messages and vague glances at school. I was scared he was going off me and the thought of that made me feel sick. I was getting so used to being with him now. It amazed me how much my feelings were growing, almost taking over.

And now he was here and looking dead cool. He was wearing a new zipped-up top, the collar turned up high. His face looked darker somehow, hard, but I liked it – it was sexy. He was jiggling his leg up and down like he was nervous, or excited – I couldn't work out which. I dropped my hand on his knee, trying to settle him. In the next room I could hear the drone of Eddie's TV. I prayed that he'd stay in his room.

"It's a real mess in here," Will said.

I smiled. I'd tidied up before he came in, so this was nothing! There was still a cup on my bedside cabinet, some clothes thrown on the chair. But it really wasn't that bad.

"If you keep things cleaner, it clears your head," he said. He pointed at some of my old cuddly toys that I pushed to the end of my bed. "Aren't you a bit old for them?"

Despite myself, I blushed. "I know it's naff, but I've had them since I was a kid. Especially Mr Snuggles."

I picked up my dog. He was small and grey-looking now. A small hole had appeared by his eye. I wasn't sure I could bear to throw him away. I'd had him for ever.

"I just thought you were cooler than that."

Will sat back on the bed, the words hanging

between us. It was like he knew that would hurt. I threw Mr Snuggles on the floor, hoping that Will would see it as an act of rebellion. In my mind, I was already packing the toys away in a bin bag, saying goodbye.

"So . . . do I get a kiss, or what?" I teased, tugging on his sleeve.

Will grinned and leant forward, not needing much persuasion. His lips were gentle at first, then much firmer. He groaned.

I jumped back. "You OK?"

"Yeah, yeah. It's just so good to have you alone – you know?"

It was then that I heard the rustle and the snigger from outside the door. I jumped up, the rage already bursting out from me.

"Eddie. . ." I hissed.

Will laughed, then whispered, "Ah, he's just doing what little brothers do. Let me have a chat."

He got up and strolled to the door before flinging it open. Eddie more or less fell straight through – all red-faced and cocky.

"All right, mate," Will said.

Eddie's expression darkened and he glared back at him.

"Can I have a quick word?" Will asked, touching his shoulder. Eddie made one of his stupid grunting noises. I think he was too shy to say anything else. Will looked over at me. His whole face was about to crack into laughter at any moment. He obviously found the whole thing hilarious. "I won't be long, Anna. Just want to get to know your brother."

They walked out of the room together, Will's arm slung casually over Eddie's shoulder. I heard them talk about the latest gaming craze before they disappeared into Eddie's room.

I sank back on to my bed, sighing. It was so typical of Eddie to ruin things just as they were getting interesting. I reached over to my bedroom drawer and pulled out the biscuits I'd hidden. I'd felt too sick to eat earlier, probably too wound up about having Will there, but now hunger clawed at my belly like a wild animal.

"Seriously – why are you eating that junk?" Will walked back into my room just as I'd taken my first bite.

I looked at him, confused, my mouth full of biscuit crumbs.

"Stuff like that is packed full of calories. I want you to look after yourself now you're with me."

"You mean you don't want me fat?" I'd swallowed and the sensation was dry and tasteless. I was no longer hungry.

"No, don't be daft. I just care about you." Will sat beside me, so close our legs were touching. "I think you're perfect as you are. I want you to stay that way."

Perfect as you are... No one had ever told me that before. I stared at the sugary crescent left in my hand, then placed it back on the cabinet to throw away later. "You're right. I should cut down on that stuff."

He squeezed my leg, smiling at me. "You know I'll help you."

Brushing away the crumbs from my jeans, I felt silly again, like I should already know this stuff – that I should already be doing it. "What did you say to Eddie?"

"Aw, we just had a chat. I told Eddie that I know what it's like to feel left out of stuff, but I asked him to respect our privacy."

"And he was cool with that?"

"Yeah – he was. Totally cool."

I shook my head. "You really must have the magic touch or something."

"So. . ." Will was picking at the thread in my duvet, not looking at me. "How were rehearsals today?"

"Good. Cool." I pushed back my hair. "Dan is dead excited – he thinks he might have a gig lined up soon. It's only another school, but it's a start."

Will looked up, his eyes catching the light. They looked almost black. "That's good, then." His voice was flat. Wrong.

"Is something up?" I said.

He shook his head softly. "It's probably nothing."

My stomach twisted. That didn't sound good. "What? What's probably nothing?"

Will looked up again and I could see his eyes were glistening. He looked like he was in pain. I took his hand in mine and squeezed it. "Will . . . tell me."

"It's just the lads; they were winding me up. Telling me that Dan fancies you. They say that the only reason he's got you in the band was to pull you."

I laughed. I couldn't help it. "Jeez, Will. That's not true. We're just really good mates. Dan's not like that."

"Isn't he?" Will reached down and pulled his

phone out of his pocket. He fiddled with it for a bit before passing it over to me. "This is what Callum forwarded to me yesterday. He wanted me to know. It's been driving me mad."

I took the mobile, feeling a bit nervous. Callum and Dan were on the same football team. They were mates. My eyes scanned the message. It was Dan's number all right.

Yeah mate, course I fancy Anna. She's a total
slag tho. Only got her in the band to score.
She can't even sing!
D

I swear my heart was thumping its way out of my chest. I felt sick. My hands were trembling holding that horrible phone, my eyes blurring as I reread the words over and over. I now knew. I knew I couldn't trust him – my mate, my best mate. Horrible. Horrible. . .

"I'm so sorry," Will whispered. "But you could see why I had to show you. I've known for a few days. I didn't know what to do. But it's been driving me mad. I hate to see you being made a mug of. It's like he's making a mug of me too."

I nodded, but I could feel the tears pricking at my eyes. I hated crying. I didn't want to do it in front of Will. He'd think I was pathetic sobbing over some loser. Some scum who I thought cared about me.

Will pulled me into his arms. I could smell his fresh aftershave, his sweet skin.

"I shouldn't have showed you," Will said, his breath tickling my neck. "I was being selfish. I was jealous. Thinking Dan could take you from me. I didn't think about how much it might hurt you."

"It's OK," I said.

"It's not. I didn't need to show you. You didn't need to see that."

"I did," I whispered. "And there's no way I'm going back now. He can find some other sucker to sing for him."

I thought of the old times in rehearsals. The laughing. The fun. The great music. I couldn't believe I'd fallen for it all. Was I so stupid to believe that I could sing? Everything Dan said to me must have been a lie, a big set-up. The band must have been laughing behind my back all the time. Thinking about it, they'd been doing that such a lot lately – like when I couldn't get the song right before. I could see them all sniggering, probably whispering about me being rubbish. Some mates! There was no way I could go back now. It would never be the same.

"Will you tell Dan that Callum told me?" Will asked. "It's just ... Callum was really worried. He didn't know what to do for the best. I mean, he didn't like you being messed about – but, you know . . . he's still Dan's mate. . ."

"I get it," I said. "You don't want Dan to know I know."

"It's not that. Of course you can tell him – it's just I don't want things to be difficult for Cal. He's a good guy."

I shook my head. "It's fine. I can't face a big scene. It's the last thing I need. I'll quietly leave. I probably need a break anyway."

Knowing Dan, he would be embarrassed about it. Maybe he'd deny it. Whatever. It wasn't worth the stress.

"You're letting him win," Will said.

"Nah," I said. "I'm letting us win."

Will hugged me harder and I tried not to let myself dissolve.

*

Half an hour before Dad was due home, I told Will he had to go. He looked at me with big sad eyes.

"You're not ashamed of me, are you?"

"No. Of course not. I'm just scared he'll kick off. I'm not sure he'll like me bringing boys home."

His eyes twinkled. "Is it something you do often?"

"Don't be daft."

I led him out, half dragging him. Eddie's door was ajar and I peered in as we passed. He was lying on his stomach on his bed. He looked asleep. I closed the door without saying a word, not wanting to disturb him.

We stepped on to the cool landing outside. There was a funny smell round here, there always was. I couldn't tell what it was, it was just *there*. The scent of Tower A. The stale air still caught my breath slightly. I could see Will taking it all in, the dusty floors, the graffiti on the walls. His eyes seemed restless.

"What's your house like?" I asked.

"Tidy," he said and, seeing me flinch, he reached out and touched my arm. "That's not a dig. It's like *crazy* tidy. Everything is packed away. Even when Mum's – well, not around – she likes things to be just right, or she gets weird."

"Will I ever get to see it?" I said.

Will circled the skin on my arm real slow. It tickled, but in a good way. "I dunno. I guess. That place kind of does my head in. I'm not sure I want to take you there. I hate being there enough myself."

"This place does me in too," I said. "But our homes – well, they're part of us, aren't they?"

"No," he said, really firmly. "We can be whatever we want to be."

He stroked my face, my cheek, my ears. I shivered with pleasure. His fingers tangled themselves in my hair. Twining around the strands and pulling them towards my face. "You should grow it really, really long," he said, tugging them slightly.

"Like Rapunzel?"

"Yeah, if you like."

He kissed me, still gripping my hair tightly in his hands. I couldn't escape, not that I wanted to. As we kissed he held on tighter, it even hurt a bit – burning at the roots – but I barely flinched.

"Thanks for tonight," he whispered as we pulled away. "It's so good having time, you know – just us."

"I know," I said.

"We need more of this."

We kissed again. It seemed like for ever. Jeez, I

wanted it to be. But I had to pull away. It was like I could hear my dad's footsteps marching up the steps. The mental clock was ticking away in my head, warning me that we were going to get caught out at any second.

"You have to go," I said.

His eyes glinted. "You shouldn't have to worry about your dad," he moaned. "Why can't we just be together?"

"It's still early days." I stroked his cheek. "Give it time."

Will kept hold of my hand for a final few seconds. His eyes were blazing into mine, so powerful that they were hard to look into, almost too uncomfortable. Then he said it.

"I love you," he said. "I bloody love you, Anna."

The words tumbled from my mouth before I could stop them.

"I love you too."

He kissed me one more time. Quicker now, barely a breath. Then he was gone.

I texted Dan that night – told him I was leaving the band for a bit. Told him I needed some time out.

He didn't reply. I guess I wasn't expecting him

to. He probably wouldn't even care. Part of me still wanted to challenge him. But most of me didn't want the stress, didn't want the embarrassment of him knowing that I knew what he thought of me. I got three messages from Will though.

Will who loved me.

Miss u so much already.

Can't wait till tomorrow. Everything is changing.

You're the only thing that matters now.

I read them all with a stupid smile on my face. I was so lucky.

He was definitely mine now. Why should I care about anything else?

You used to tell me that someone special would completely rock my world. I used to laugh at you then. Well, guess what, it's happened. I'm finding it hard to take the cheesy grin off my face right now.

She'll do anything for me, anything.

She's perfect. ☺

Funny how I'm not missing you quite so much now. Funny how Mum's moods aren't bugging me quite so much.

Funny how I don't really give a crap any more.

The morning after Will told me he loved me, I had five messages waiting for me. And two pictures. One where he looked soulful, a bit lost. In the second, he was staring right at the lens, right at me – and was smiling. He never smiled in photos. I could see the light in his eyes, the sweet curve in his lips. It made me want to be with him so much, to kiss him again.

"Urgh."

I spun round to find Eddie behind me, a typical smug expression plastered on his face. I shoved the phone back into my pocket. "It's none of your business," I hissed.

"It's gross, man," Eddie said, his nose screwed up. "Seriously, you two make me feel sick."

"*You* make me feel sick." I shoved past him and into the living room. Dad was up already and sitting in front of the TV, munching toast.

"You two arguing again?" he said, his eyes not leaving the screen.

"She can't take a joke!" Eddie said, flopping down next to him. "What are we doing today anyway?"

I watched my dad's face. His expression barely changed. When was the last time we did anything together at the weekend? He was either too tired or too busy.

"Shall we go into town?" Eddie continued. "I need new trainers."

Dad sniffed. "Yeah, all right."

"Great day out. . ." I muttered, slinking past the pair of them.

"That's enough of your attitude!" Dad yelled. "It wouldn't hurt you to come along."

But I'd already left the room. I had better things to do.

The Swamp was so hot, sticky and sultry. Even in the shade, I could feel the damp heat melting into my skin. I kept shifting on the grass, paranoid that I was turning into a lobster or even worse, stinking of BO.

"You OK?" Will was watching me, a lazy smile

stretched on his tanned face. He looked even better in the heat, which didn't seem fair somehow.

I twisted my hair into a ponytail, desperate to get some breeze on to my neck. I tipped my head back. There really was no air, not a breath. Even the tree that we were sitting under seemed to be drooping, caving in due to the lack of moisture.

"Aw, don't do that," he moaned, reaching forward. "You know I love your hair the way it is."

I dropped my hand again, sighing. Wet hair stuck against my neck again. Nice.

"You seem fed up?" he said.

"It's nothing," I said. "Just my dad, Eddie, the usual."

"What's he been doing now?"

"He's just so stressed. He has a go for no reason. Even if I do stuff, he has a go. It's driving me mad. He seems madder than usual."

I thought back to this morning, to all the yelling. To Dad's angry face as he threw the dirty cereal bowl into the sink. The one bowl that I forgot to wash up. I seriously felt like I was losing grip of what was normal now.

Will laid back a little, looked up towards the sky. I could see the strong angle of his jaw, the beginning of his stubble. His mouth was working gently, chewing on some gum.

"I keep telling you – you shouldn't worry about him. You have me now, I'll look after you," he said.

"I know, but. . ."

"No buts, just give me time." His eyes were closed now against the sun. He looked so relaxed, chilled. "You should spend less time there, screw him."

I nodded. Less time in that poky flat certainly sounded appealing, especially now that Eddie had his mates round all the time, trashing the place and expecting me to sort it out. Maybe if Dad had to face it alone, he'd appreciate me more. Maybe he'd have a go at Eddie then, sort him out a bit.

"I'll come and live at yours," I joked.

One eye opened. "I doubt my mum would even notice. She's pretty much away with the fairies." He smiled, wide and happy. "Maybe I'll bring you round one day. You can see what a loon she is." He half laughed, his hand batting the grass beside him.

My heart was beating so rapidly now. This was a real result. This had to mean Will trusted me enough to even be thinking about it. I tried to fight back the urge to hug him hard.

"See," he said, like he'd read my mind. "That's how important you are to me. Even Zak and Callum don't come to my house. I want you to see that you're special to me, that you get to see my entire life."

Even if it hadn't had been thirty-one degrees, I would still have been sweating at that point. Internally, I churned over what he'd just said – wondered just what I was going to be exposed to. Was his mum really that bad? Will didn't feed me much information about her, but the little bits he said were negative and cool. Most of the time his face went tight and cold, like he was talking about something that disgusted him.

"But remember, all we need is each other," he continued, lacing his fingers through the grass. "Everyone else will just distract us. Cause problems. It will only get worse, especially once they see how close we are. All we need is us, not interference from people that don't get it."

"Of course, I know that."

"So why are you still seeing that stupid counsellor?" he asked suddenly, turning to face me.

"I – I, well, they wanted me to. . ."

"Who? The school? You don't need it, Anna. You're not some nutcase. You've not got mental problems. You don't need someone poking about in your stuff, asking you about your life."

"It's quite helpful," I said softly, thinking about the last time, about Debs' encouraging words. About the family tree we'd drawn up together. About the feelings I'd conjured up around Dad, how we'd talked through how stressed and tired he must be feeling too.

"Helpful?" He sat up, glaring at me. "Jeez, Anna, are you a mug or something? I said before, they just want to tick their little boxes. Do you really think they care about you? This is their job. What they're paid to do!"

"I think Debs does want. . ."

Will grabbed my arm, hard, pinching the skin. I breathed in, shocked at his strength. I wanted to shake him off, but he gripped me tighter.

"She doesn't give a CRAP about you," he hissed. Then he released me and sank back, sighing.

I moved away a little, rubbing my skin. My arm was red, white stripes glaring up at me where his fingers had been. An imprint. I was shocked, a little shaken. Had he meant to grab me so hard?

"I'm sorry," Will said, staring at the ground, playing with the grass again. "I'm so sorry. I just wish you'd listen to me. I know this stuff. You have to trust me."

I looked up into his big wide eyes. "You shouldn't hold me like that," I whispered.

"I only did it because you wouldn't listen," he said. "You know I'd never hurt you."

I shook my head, not sure, still rubbing the streaked skin.

"You just know how to wind me up," he said. "You get to me."

"I wasn't trying to," I said.

He touched my cheek, soft now, tender, nothing like before. "I love you. I love you so much."

I blinked. Smiled. Of course.

Of course he did.

It got so hot by the late afternoon, I couldn't stand it any longer.

"I'm sticking my feet in."

Will looked at me, mouth held in a smirk. "Really? You know it's truly bogging in there!"

"Yeah, so? I want to cool my feet down."

"Cool them down? They'll probably rot off! You'll catch a disease or something." He was laughing. "Fair enough, go in – but don't say I didn't warn you!"

I stuck my tongue out. What did I care? I kicked off my shoes and stepped forward. Yeah, OK, the water was a weird brown-green colour and, yeah, there was unknown stuff drifting around in there; but my feet were swelling in the heat. I just wanted one or two minutes to cool them down.

As I stepped in, Will yelled with pleasure. "You are seriously rank!" he declared.

"It's not so bad," I said, letting the silt settle. It was cool. Nice. The mud under my toes was soothing.

"Tramp!" he said. "Hey! Look at me!"

I looked over my shoulder and he clicked a photo on his phone. Then another. "I'm posting this," he said. "I'm telling everyone my girlfriend swims in bogs!"

"I'll splash you!" I said, grinning back. I poked one foot out. Dark weeds clung to it.

He laughed, walking over. "Doesn't it smell?"

"Not really." I moved my feet around a bit, feeling them sink a little more. "I just think there's loads of mud in here. Mud's good for you, isn't it?"

"If you're a worm. . ." He bent forward and stuck his hand in. "It is cool!"

"See!"

He was so quick, like a cat. His hand shot up and

sloshed a load of water over me, and then again. I gasped in shock and kicked back, getting his hair wet. He splashed me again.

"You pig!" I spat.

He plucked something green from his hair, kneeling back on the bank. "I couldn't resist, sorry."

"But my top . . . I'm soaked!"

It wasn't even a top I could get away with. It was white and now it was wet and clinging against my bra, showing it all. I hugged my chest, cringing. Suddenly I wasn't hot any more. I wanted a jumper on. Or a coat. Anything.

"I'm sorry," he said, "I really am. I couldn't resist."

"My dad will kill me."

Without another word, Will pulled off his T-shirt. I'd only caught him a bit around the neck, so he was still dry. I couldn't help but stare. His chest was pale but firm, nice. I looked away quickly. I still felt embarrassed, like I shouldn't be seeing him like that. Not yet anyway.

"You can wear this," he said. "It'll just look big on you. Take yours off though; otherwise it will soak that too."

I took the top nervously, "Will—"

"I'll look away, I promise," he said, turning.

I stepped out of the water carefully. I didn't look at him. I couldn't. I quickly peeled off the damp top and threw it on to the grass. Then, fumbling, clumsy and feeling exposed, I pulled on his dark top. It engulfed me. Smelt of him. His aftershave and a little of his sweat.

I turned and he was facing me, smiling. "Nice," he said. "Really nice."

His phone was in his hand and he shoved it into his back pocket, winking.

"You look so good," he said softly.

I smiled back, but inside I was cringing, wondering how much he saw.

It was gone seven by the time I got back to the flat. I was already on edge. I knew Dad wanted me home sooner. I opened the front door carefully and slipped into the hall. I still had Will's top on and I clung to the material, wishing that he was there with me.

Dust motes were bopping about in the late evening light. The entire place was starting to smell. Not really bad, just a bit dusty and sour. The vacuum cleaner lay discarded by Dad's bedroom door, the hose wrapped loosely around its neck like a noose. I think Dad started it a few weeks ago and then gave up. Like most things.

I couldn't see them at first. Then I did. They were snuggled up on the sofa together, watching some film. Dad's arm was slung round Eddie's neck. Eddie had a mouthful of something. As my eyes flickered downwards I saw the discarded pizza box on the floor. Neither of them bothered to look up at me.

"You're back, then," Dad said, eyes still fixed on the screen. I could see his jaw was locked.

"I'm sorry, I—"

"Don't tell me. The bus was late, or you forgot the time, or you had to rescue some stranger from a near death experience." Dad turned. His large brown eyes just looked sad.

"I'm sorry."

Dad shook his head and looked away again. I noticed he was flexing and unflexing the hand that was resting on the sofa. For a minute that held me in a trance. I wondered if he'd ever hurt anyone with it. He was a big man. An ex-boxer. Surely he could, if he wanted to.

I glanced at my arm, turning it slightly. The marks had gone, of course, but it was like I could still feel them burning. I could still imagine Will gripping my skin. I shook the image away. I was being silly. Melodramatic. Typical of me. The whole thing was my fault anyway. Mine.

I'd upset him.

Eddie kept on eating, red sauce smeared all over his face. I longed to ask for a piece, but there was no way I was going to. Instead I kicked the box. I couldn't help myself. "You've eaten, then," I said.

Dad didn't flinch. "You weren't home. Your brother was hungry. What did you expect us to do?"

"Yeah!" said Eddie, grinning. "I was starving."

"You could've waited. You must've known I'd want to eat too."

Dad's voice was cold and eerily slow. "I don't know anything any more, Anna, because you don't bother to tell me. I don't know what you're up to these days."

"What do you mean by that?"

"I mean, when were you going to tell me about this boyfriend of yours?"

I froze. I think my heart actually stopped. I blinked. Then I turned to Eddie, who was still grinning smugly. "You swore you wouldn't tell," I hissed.

"Yeah, well. . ." He shrugged. "What's the point? I thought Dad should know."

"You little. . ."

"Anna!" Dad's voice cut across mine. "Don't take this out on him. I'm glad he told me. At least I know now why you've been sneaking about everywhere."

"I was going to tell you," I said. "It's not a big deal. You'll like Will – he's cool."

Dad glared back at me. "How old is he?"

"Sixteen. So?"

"And you met at school?"

"Yes." I wanted to laugh then. "Why is that better or worse than picking up some lad on the estate?"

"It's no better, Anna. You've still been lying to me." He sighed. "You're grounded anyway. I'm sick of the lateness and the constant lying. I'll have to think about this Will. I'm not sure. . ."

I snorted. "Grounded? I'm fourteen, not five!"

"And you can lose the attitude too!" he shouted. "What, do you think now you've got some smarty-pants bloke, you can talk to me like scum?"

"Well, you are, aren't you?"

The words flew from my lips. Eddie gasped. I could see Dad sit back, like I'd shoved him. I suppose I might as well have.

"Get to your room," he said coldly.

"I wish Mum was here. It's your fault. You couldn't keep her, could you?"

Dad flapped at me. His eyes were lost somewhere. "Go on. Just go. I can't look at you right now."

"Loser!" I yelled, as I turned on my heel and slammed myself into my bedroom.

I threw myself on the bed. Those stupid cuddly toys were there and I chucked them all on the floor, kicking them into the far corner. Except Mr Snuggles – Mum's present to me. I kept him in my hands for a minute longer. I remembered when she'd given him to me. How different things were then.

With clawing fingers I ripped out his stupid, loving eyes. Then I threw him on to the discarded heap.

I wasn't their kid any more.

I remember a lot of stuff.

I remember that Lego thing I built as a kid – do you? Great big space station. So cool, revolving doors, proper towers. Took me days. Then Mum smashed it up because you wanted her to.

Do you remember?

I only had it for an afternoon. All that work for nothing. Yet while it lasted, it had been the best thing ever...

That's what happens when you have something good. People try to wreck it. People like you, like Mum.

I have Anna, but she doesn't understand it yet. She doesn't see how much I love her. I think she will get it in the end though.

As for Mum – ha! A corner has been turned. That's what they think anyway. She's talking again. She's met some group on the internet and she's on there all the time. She told me she's healing.

She's trying to forgive.

But she still looks at me like I'm nothing.

I'm still not you.

I walked from the bus stop to school feeling like a lead weight was tied tightly to my neck. The whole weekend had been spent being largely ignored by Dad. And now I was grounded. Will would hate that. It was so pathetic, made me look like some little girl who had no control over her own life.

He'd never want to be with me now.

It was bad enough that I'd had to make up excuses to him on Sunday, pretending I felt ill and couldn't see him. We had meant to be going bowling. We had meant to be together. I could hear the disappointment in his voice. Disappointment that had quickly flicked to something else. Repulsion?

"Just get better soon, yeah," he'd said. "I'll find something to do."

All evening, I'd imagined him out with his mates, having fun. Flirting. I kept checking my phone – but

I had no messages from him. I checked online and saw that he'd posted pictures. Loads of them.

Having a laugh with good mates, he'd posted.

Him with his mates. But girls were there. In one picture his arm was around one of them. She was pretty, much prettier than me. They were both laughing. My stomach twisted in jealousy.

I miss you, I'd texted, a little later that evening.

I'd got nothing back.

Not a word.

"Hey!"

I looked up, expecting, hoping, to see Will. But it wasn't. It was Dan.

"Hey," I said back. I knew my voice sounded flat. I didn't care.

Dan stood in front of me, arms to his side, looking a little – well, unsure. He tipped his head a bit, letting his floppy fringe fall into his eyes. "So. Why the text? What have I done to make you leave the band?"

"Why do you think it's you?" I said, walking past him. "I just need a break."

"But it makes no sense, Anna. We're getting so far. You know that. We can't stop now."

Irritation clawed at me. "Just leave it," I hissed.

But Dan was following me. He never could let stuff go. "It's him, isn't it? Will. What has he said?"

I spun round. I was pretty sure steam would start to come out of my skin. "Why? Jealous, are you?"

Dan froze. Then a snide smile slid across his face. He shook his head slowly. "Sheesh."

"I'm right, aren't I? You're jealous because of Will."

Dan's eyes were twinkling like they always did, but it was different this time; they seemed colder. "Yeah, OK, Anna, hands up. You've sussed me out."

"You're sick," I said.

He made a noise, a half laugh, and stepped back. "In that case, maybe it *is* better if you did leave the group. To be honest, I could do without the dramas."

I nodded. Walked away again – only this time I felt like the lead weight had gained six friends.

"Did you have fun yesterday?"

I couldn't help asking. The question had been floating inside me all day.

We were sitting at the corner of the school field. It was like our place. Quiet and chilled. Will was leant against the metal fence and I was laid across his legs, happily munching the strawberries he'd brought from home. If I closed my eyes I could pretend I wasn't in school. Maybe we were in a deserted paradise of our own, far away from everybody. I was with him. That was all that mattered.

"It was cool hanging out with everyone again," Will said.

"It looked fun."

"It was," Will replied. "Shame you were ill."

"You didn't text."

"I was busy – you know, it was a busy night."

I licked the juice from my lips and considered this for a bit. Was I being silly? "Did you get my message?" I asked softly.

"Yeah, of course. It was nice." He shuffled a little. "I meant to reply, but you know how it is. . ."

"At least your mates still like you. . ." I said.

"What? Do you mean Izzy? I might have a word with her, you know."

I sat up. "And say what?"

"I'm not sure yet. I could say loads of things – 'get a life' would be one, or . . . oh . . . there's a thought. . ."

I sat up a little. Will looked like he was lost in his own world, but that sly little grin was snaking across his face.

"What?" I said, poking him. "What's a thought?"

"Maybe she's a lesbian. Maybe she's got the hots for you. Can't bear to let you go."

"Don't be daft! That's not the reason."

"Why not? She's got no fella of her own and seems to be deeply affected by you having one. Either that, or she's just a jealous screw-up."

"Maybe I should see a bit more of her; she is my mate," I reasoned.

Will snorted. "Feel free, if that's how you want to waste your spare time. It's not like we have bags of it. Don't you think I could be seeing the lads more? Don't you think I've made sacrifices too?"

"Sorry, I didn't mean it to sound like that."

"Nah. It's OK. I'm just saying – going out with someone is like that, isn't it? You just want to be with them all the time."

I nodded. "Yeah – all the time."

"I'm sure Izzy will get that, one day."

I nodded, said, "Maybe," and reached into my bag for my crisps.

"Aw, babe. You know how I feel about that stuff."

Will sighed. "If you eat junk like that, your body will turn to junk. You know that. . ."

I thought of the pretty girl he'd had his arm round last night. She was really thin. Would he hate me if I was bigger? "I wasn't thinking," I muttered, putting them back, trying to ignore the empty feeling inside.

"You're amazing," he said softly. "Have I told you that?"

"Not enough," I said, flashing him a cheeky grin.

"Well, you are, and I'll keep telling you every time I see you."

"Anyway," I said, lying back down, "it looks like I won't be seeing you all the time now."

"What?" He sat up, jolting me. "What do you mean?"

"I mean, Dad knows. Eddie snitched on us. So now I'm grounded. I don't even know how long for. Dad's not even talking to me."

Will took in a deep breath, but said nothing.

"It'll be all right," I said, stroking his chest. "After a few weeks of being the best daughter, he'll change his mind – I'm sure."

"It's not all right though, is it?" Will said coolly.

"It is what it is. What can I do? I live there. I have to go along with it."

"No," he said, gripping my hand in his. "No, you don't. You have to listen to me." He smiled, that half smile that I could never quite work out was cold or charming.

"I know exactly what we need to do."

Will walked me back to class as he always did, right to the door. We lingered for a bit just in the doorway. He was always a little more casual in public, didn't like to hold my hand for too long or be over the top. He didn't want to give people reason to take the mick.

As we stood talking, Dan passed. Immediately I cringed. I'd been avoiding places where I knew he'd be – not wanting another confrontation. It didn't help that Will had told me he'd heard that they were looking to recruit a new singer already. It was obvious I was that easy to replace.

Dan was walking on the other side of the corridor with some mates, people I didn't really know. He saw us and hesitated. I think he was going to say something. His eyes fell on mine and his mouth opened and he moved towards me. Then he saw Will and seemed to step back.

I felt Will stiffen next to me. Dan glanced at me again. Then suddenly he blew me a kiss. His mates laughed and started ribbing him, but Dan was still staring at me, not smiling at all. That wasn't like him to look so serious. Something shifted inside me, a really uneasy feeling. Then Dan shook his head sadly and moved on.

"What's his problem?" Will hissed.

"Nothing. He just looked over, that's all."

But Will was still watching him, his face tight. "He's winding me up," he said.

I looked down at his hands. They were clenched so tight, the knuckles were turning white.

Will wanted to get the bus home again with me, but I said no. It seemed daft, him going all that way just to see me to the door. It wasn't dark. I knew I would be fine.

I could see him mulling it over. "I like making sure you're safe," he said.

"And I will be. Honestly, I'll be fine," I said, squeezing his arm. "You could meet up with Zak or something? You don't need me around all the time."

He nodded, then smiled. "Yeah. You're right," he

said. "As long as you're sure, then." He kissed me lightly on top of the head.

Seeing him walk away in the opposite direction was quite a relief. I had a headache. I felt tired. I just wanted to be on my own for a bit. Plus I kept thinking about stuff that happened earlier in the day. Will had seemed wound up over nothing. So what if Dan was flirting with me? Knowing Dan, it was probably all a joke anyway.

My thoughts tumbled through our times in rehearsals. I could still feel the beat of the music, the heat of the room, the intense vibe that only we – the band – understood. I missed the banter, the laughter, the raw energy that we'd had. But how could I ever it get it back now?

I had really thought Dan was my mate, someone I'd known for ever. Just thinking about what he'd done made my heart ache. I felt torn, like parts of my soul had been ripped out. Something was missing. Did he really mean what he'd said on that text, or had he been messing around? Maybe I should talk to him – find out what the message was all about?

But Will? I'd be betraying Will, wouldn't I? Letting him down? He hated what Dan had done as much as I did. He said it made him look like a mug, too.

I waited for the bus, leaning against the shelter, churning my options over and over. My eyes felt heavy and dry – I think I could have probably slept right there. I didn't notice Lyn coming towards me. Not until he was right next to me.

"Hi," he said, smiling. "You OK?"

I turned. Then checked myself. Lyn didn't go to St Nick's. He went to Perryfield High, by our estate. "Hey, what are you doing here?"

"Fancied a change of scene," he laughed. "Nah. I had an interview for the sixth form here."

I smiled. It made sense – he looked more smartly dressed than usual – in dark trousers and short-sleeved white shirt. I had to admit he looked pretty good, his skin darker than usual against the pale material, his hair cropped short and his eyes, so ice cool – gleaming right at me.

"How did it go?" I asked.

"OK, I think . . . I dunno really. I mean, they seem pretty uptight here. They probably don't want a kid from the Mac ruining their reputation."

"I'm a kid from the Mac!" I laughed.

"Yeah – but you're obviously different. You're

like Jess, my girlfriend. You make an effort, don't you? You can fit in anywhere."

I shrugged. "I guess. . ."

"Actually, Jess is the reason I'm here. Before her, I wasn't bothered about school at all. Barely showed up. But she made me see I was wasting my chance," he laughed. "Turns out I have a brain in my head after all!"

"That's cool," I said. "It's good she had that impact on you."

"Yeah – yeah it is." He was grinning now. It made me grin too; it was kind of addictive.

"And you're with that guy? The one I see you with round the estate sometimes?"

"Yes, Will."

"He looks familiar – I don't know why." Lyn's face screwed up a little. "What's his name again?"

"Will, Will Bennett. I don't think you'd know him."

"Nah. . . I dunno, there's something. It might come to me."

I smiled. "He's cool. I really like him."

Lyn touched my arm. "Nice one, Anna. I'm pleased for you."

The bus approached. A breeze of warm engine

fumes blew grit in our faces. The doors creaked open and Lyn gestured for me to step in. He followed me, guiding me, his hand gently on the middle of my back.

We sat together, but didn't talk any more. Lyn's phone rang and I assumed it was Jess, as his voice went soft and sweet and he turned away from me slightly. All I could hear was his low, murmuring words. It was oddly comforting. It made me want to sleep. I gazed out of the smoky window. The day had been long and every part of me ached.

I thought of Dan earlier. Of his reaction when I told him he was jealous of Will. Surely he'd have denied it if it wasn't true? Why was I tearing myself up over this? It wasn't worth the energy. I had Will. I should be happy. I didn't need the stupid band any more.

But I still couldn't fight back the sadness, watching as the streets and cars flashed beside me, wondering if I ever really knew Dan at all.

Was I really that bad a judge of character?

Two hours later, I was back home, curled on my bed, trying to ignore the loud music that Eddie was playing. I was so exhausted I couldn't even be bothered to argue with him.

My phone bleeped and I instantly felt a spark of excitement. It was Will. My fingers stumbled over the keys, keen to open it.

Only this time, the words were so blunt and cruel they tore right through my heart.

> You've been mugging me off. I saw you with that guy from your estate earlier. Pretty cosy, hey!
> No wonder you wanted me gone.
> We're done.

My brain was slow, trying to figure out what he meant. Then it hit me. Lyn.

Will thought I'd been with Lyn.

It was so crazy I almost laughed out loud. Seriously, how could he think that!

I tried to call but the phone flipped straight to voicemail. I sent him a text, begging him to contact me – but I knew he wouldn't.

He'd got it all wrong and all I could think was I had to get him back.

I had to sort this out.

LIES! I can't stand the bloody lies.

I went home. Straight home. Mum was there. In the kitchen, trying to clean the oven. Stupid smile on her face, fixed there like it was painted on. I yelled at her, I can't even remember what, yelled right in her face. She barely flinched. Just kept cleaning and humming.

If I told you what I did next – would you be shocked? Would you care?

I slapped her.

I think she stopped humming then.

I didn't stick around, to be honest. My hand was stinging. I was gone. Back out.

I stayed with Zak again last night. They don't care who sleeps there. Perhaps I should move in?

I texted Anna and told her it was over. I hate her so much for making me do that. She must want this. She's playing games with me. I'm not having it.

I hate it that I still see her face when I close my eyes.

Eddie was hammering at my door. "C'mon. Get up. We'll be late."

I pulled myself up. My sheets felt sticky and smelly, the room was far too hot. Everything was just where I'd left it – phone on the bed. Book discarded, unread on the cabinet, clothes all over the floor. I'd slept for probably four hours. My brain just couldn't turn off, and my stomach kept churning.

I felt awful; my head was really hurting and my eyes still felt dry and small. I glanced at the time and realized I only had ten minutes or so to get ready.

"Anna, are you up yet?" Eddie's voice, although still whiny, sounded concerned, so I flung open the door. He stood there, looking sheepish – hair sticking up all over the place, jam smeared around his lips.

"You've eaten, then?" I said.

"I made some toast." He looked proud of himself.

I stood there staring at him, not able to think clearly. My brain was just full of: *Will dumped you. You screwed up. It's over.*

"Are you OK? You look kind of weird."

"I'm not going into school today, I feel sick," I said. "Are you OK walking yourself?"

"Sure. I'll just knock for Kelvin."

I nodded. Usually Eddie and I parted at the bus stop. Dad liked us to walk some of the way together. But it was only a five-minute walk to the junior school. I knew he'd be fine.

Eddie's eyes met mine; he was chewing his lip and looking kind of awkward. For a minute I saw a flash of Mum. That was something she would always do.

"Are you sure you're OK, though?" he said. "Should I wake Dad up or something?"

"I'm fine, honest. I just need to sleep." I touched his head, soft curls like candyfloss under my skin. I realized all I wanted to do was cry.

I turned my phone off and buried myself under the duvet again, drinking in the slightly salty scent of my sweat. I was rank. I needed a shower. But I couldn't move. I felt heavy and useless.

In the end I think I slept for an hour or so, waking with a thicker head and a dry throat. I eased myself up and padded out into the kitchen to get some water. To my surprise, Dad was already up – sitting at the table, reading some kind of letter. He looked sad.

"All right?" I approached him carefully, worried he still hated me.

Dad looked up, but it was like he couldn't quite see me. His eyes looked all misty and wrong. He sniffed and drew a hand across them. "Anna? What are you doing here? It's not teacher training day again, is it?"

"I don't feel good," I said. At least this wasn't a lie. I felt awful.

"Oh." He looked unsure of what to say.

"I just have a headache. I'll be OK."

I went to the sink and poured some water. It was a struggle to drink, like my whole throat had closed up. I kept thinking of Will and my stomach flipped, but not in a good way. He'd be in school. He'd probably already moved on. I stared into my glass. Perhaps he'd never liked me that much anyway? Maybe that evening with his friends was all he needed to realize things weren't working out. This was the only thing that made sense. I hadn't flirted with Lyn. Will must have used that as an excuse, the perfect reason to end things.

"You look white," Dad said softly. "Like you've seen a ghost. Do you need to eat something?"

I shook my head. "I feel sick."

"Make sure you eat something soon."

"I will."

"And don't think this means I've forgotten everything. I'm not falling for any pathetic little-girl act. You're still grounded. I still want you here with us – not messing around with that boy of yours."

"It's not an act," I hissed. I tried to ignore the gnawing pain inside me that started the minute he brought Will into it.

"Whatever. You just need to remember in my house, you follow my rules."

I said nothing. There was nothing to say.

Dad's head dipped a little. He took the letter that he was holding and carefully folded it. "I was thinking, Anna – we really need to sort out access with your mum. . ."

"Access?" I looked at him, confused.

"You know. Times when you and Eddie go to see her. She's your mum – no matter what she's done, you need her."

"No," I said. I took another gulp of water and tipped the rest down the sink, watching it spin down the plughole. "I'm not interested."

"Maybe when you feel better we can talk about it? I think Eddie wants it – and your mum does."

"Does she?" I spat the words out.

"Yes, of course. She said so when she spoke to me last, and this letter says the same. She knows you're angry – well, we all are, aren't we – but she wants to be part—"

"She can go to hell!" I yelled, smashing the glass into the sink.

I didn't realize I'd broken it, not at first, but I heard Dad gasp and then saw the blood on my hands. Blood and sparkling shards on my skin.

"Anna. . ." Dad was spluttering now. "My poor girl. Are you OK?"

Tiny cuts on my hand, but nothing felt as bad as the pain inside.

"Why am I getting it so wrong?" he said softly.

I watched as he staggered towards me, his face open in shock. I was shaking.

He wrapped me in his arms.

*

Back in my bed, I was knocked out for hours. It was like I'd been sleep-deprived for days. My body seemed to want to be shut down from it all, my mind locked away. I pulled the covers over my head and lay fully clothed in the stale heat. Broken, confusing dreams fractured my sleep, but it didn't matter.

At least I wasn't thinking.

I woke to the thud of the front door. I knew then that Dad had left for work. Loneliness crept up on me like a cold ghost. I sat up slowly, unfolding my heavy legs. Glancing at my clock, I saw that Eddie wouldn't be home for another hour.

The flat felt so empty. So did I.

And then I saw him. At the end of my bed was Mr Snuggles. His beady eyes had been fixed and were gleaming up at me. I could see the thread was wonky, and an end dangled untidily where it hadn't been finished off. If I breathed hard enough, I could still faintly smell Dad's aftershave in the room.

I pulled the stupid toy towards me and cried.

"You'll never guess what?"

Eddie strolled in, throwing his bag across the

room. I glared back at him. Most of his gossip was too dull for words. The stupid quiz show on TV was bound to be more interesting.

"That mate of yours. Dan? He got beaten up yesterday," he said anyway, eyes shining. He thumped his fist into his hand, as if to make the point.

"Dan?" I blinked. "Are you sure?"

"Everyone's talking about it. Apparently a gang jumped him after school. Smashed his face and mashed up his hand." Eddie frowned "Man, that's harsh. He plays guitar, doesn't he?"

I nodded mutely, my head spinning. "Do they know who it was?"

"Everyone says he upset someone on the Mac. Been flirting with their girl. It was arranged, apparently, to teach him a lesson."

I thought of Lyn and my head started to spin. Why had he really been at the bus stop? Was the interview a lie? Maybe Dan had upset him?

Or Will? I pushed the thought away. No, Will wasn't like that. He wasn't a fighter.

"His poor hand though," I breathed. I looked down at the tiny cuts on my own palm and felt sick.

"He's totally screwed!" Eddie said, the excitement

clear in his voice. "Anyway, what you cooking? I'm starving."

I guess I wasn't expecting much. By the evening I was zoned out on my bed, music playing, watching bland videos on the internet. I couldn't focus on schoolwork. I couldn't focus on anything. I debated messaging Dan, to check that he was OK, but quickly decided against it. I was probably the last person he wanted to hear from. And what could I say? *Hope you feel better soon? Hey, sorry to hear about your hand...* Everything was so rubbish and difficult.

When my phone buzzed, I actually jolted. Then when I saw Will's name there, my stomach flipped.

The message was stark and simple. I reread it at least ten times, my heart thumping.

> If you want this to work out, meet me in an hour – by the bus stop.
>
> If you're not there – it's over.

I knew what I had to do.

Funny how things seem clearer after a good sleep. Or even a bad sleep. . . I was tossing and turning quite a bit, thoughts all over the place. I just want things to work out in my life. I'm sick of everything going off track.

I tried to ignore Mum this morning. Jeez, she even tried to make me breakfast. I was like, "You haven't made me breakfast for years and here you are trying to serve up cornflakes – get a grip." She was all wobbly-lipped and "I'm just trying, that's all." She got more cereal on the floor than in the bowl. It's so sad, it's funny. She ended up crying again, proper wailing.

I tried to make her toast, butter it right up like she used to have it. But she smashed the plate on the floor. Bloody toast everywhere. I picked up the knife and pointed it at her. I said stuff. Stuff she deserves. She just kept staring at the blade, like she thought I'd stab her or something.

Maybe I wanted to.

What's the point of HER? We all know she's a wreck, a shell of whatever she once was. We all know she hasn't got it in her to change – she keeps saying she will, but it NEVER HAPPENS.

We all know she just wants you back. You. No one else

will do. I'm like the rubbish, the second-hand copy. I'm the one she'd like to throw away.

It doesn't matter how much of a dick you were – she wants you back.

I walked away then, like I always do. I just disappear.

I still had a blade in my hand and all I kept thinking was:

I want the rage to go.

So, slipping out was easy enough. Eddie was asleep pretty early, his headphones still clamped to his ears. Usually I'd turn his music off. But not tonight. Dad was due back just after ten, another hour away. I had no idea how long Will wanted to see me for, so I had to cover my tracks. Luckily my stuffed animals formed a pretty good "body" shape under the duvet. I spent ages moulding it, getting it just right.

I placed the spare key in my pocket and left quickly, closing the door as carefully as I could, holding my breath as it made a gentle click. I didn't like leaving Eddie on his own, but he was ten – not a baby. Besides, what other choice did I have?

It wasn't until I was outside the flat, in the stale stairway, that I realized I had just five minutes. Will liked me to be on time. Being late meant you didn't care. If I wasn't there on the hour, he'd go, no question.

I never normally used the knackered lifts, but for speed I chose to this time. As the steel doors growled open, I tried not to breathe in the stench of piss, dirt and general decay. Even the buttons were caked in grime, chewing gum wedged in the grooves. The floor was sticky and dark. I pressed G and closed my eyes as the lift juddered into life, protesting all the way. I counted silently, listening to the thundering of the blood in my ears. I knew I couldn't panic. I was better than that. I knew I could do it. I knew I had to.

I was trapped in the lift two years ago. It was a Saturday afternoon and I had just come back from getting milk for Mum. The lift ground to a halt between the fourth and fifth floor. I was stuck. It sounds silly now, because it could only have been a few minutes before the lift jolted into action again, but I remember thinking I would be stuck in that grey cage for hours. By the time I got out, I was shaking, with that nasty smell drowning my pores.

Yet here I was again, biting my lip, counting the time in my head, praying for the doors to open. When they did, I almost puked with relief.

I flew out of the tower into the cool night, passing two blokes who were huddled together, smoking. They shouted after me, but I ignored them.

I got to the bus stop in seconds, my heart beating so hard I thought it would burst out of my throat. I doubled up, catching my breath. Dry, hacking air.

I was on time. But he wasn't there.

I felt stupid, just standing there staring at the chipped plastic seats. Will was never late. Never. I reached for my phone and wondered if I should call. That would look needy.

Outside the tower, a small gang had collected. This was normal. The main guys, the older ones, stood like gatekeepers at the foot of the towers. Others swarmed around in small packs, dark jackets zipped up high, trainers glistening bright. Some were on bikes, doing wheelies or just circling slowly. Others sat on the small wall, or ran around the perimeter of the block, smoking, laughing, shouting. One or two, like stray wasps, hung around inside the main foyers, thumbing the buttons on the lifts, kicking the walls and swearing at anyone that dared to pass.

Most people stayed away at night.

I thought of Dan. Who had he upset on the Mac? It was pretty common for small packs to hunt out lads that had upset one of them. I was surprised I'd not heard any gossip. Had I been too involved with Will to notice? I thought of Lyn's smiling face and wondered if he'd been involved. A shiver ran through me.

"All right?"

I turned, startled, almost not recognizing him in his dark jacket and hat. "Will. I thought you weren't coming."

He shrugged. "Sorry. I was held up."

He looked different somehow, pale. Dark shadows lined his eyes like bruises.

"You wanna stay here?" My eyes wandered back to the pack of boys. They probably hadn't noticed us, especially with Will dressed the way he was, but I didn't want to risk any hassle.

"Nah, let's just walk."

I nodded and we set off, kind of shuffling at slow speed. I followed him as he took us down the side road. It led towards the park. Not much of a park really, but it was OK.

"You got out, then," he said. "I wondered if you'd bother."

"Of course I'd bother. It's not as easy as that."

"You weren't in school."

"You noticed, then?"

"Of course I noticed!" He sounded hurt. "Was it because of me?"

I dipped my head. "Yeah, I guess. . ."

He sniffed. Then suddenly he pulled towards my hand. We'd reached the end of the road now and were facing the fields. It looked odd in the dark, too black. We stood for a bit, just staring.

"Hey." He stroked the skin, the rough cuts still sore. "What have you done?"

"It's nothing . . . a glass broke."

His finger continued to brush over the wounds. "You need to be more careful," he said tightly.

"Sorry. . ."

"I don't want us to be over," he said finally. "But I have to trust you."

"You can," I said.

He squeezed my hand, tight. I flinched. "This is really important. If I let you in, you can't mess me around."

"I wouldn't." The pressure on my hand was intense; he was strong. I wriggled a bit but I didn't think he'd noticed. "Will, you're hurting. It's still sore."

"Am I?" The words floated between us before he released his grip. I flexed my hand, feeling it pulse and burn. "You hurt *me*," he hissed. "You did that to me."

"I didn't do anything," I said. "You saw me with Lyn. We met by chance. I didn't even know he'd be there that day."

Will sighed. "I want to trust you, I do. But can you blame me? You tell me to go and then I see you with another guy and he has his hand around you—"

"He didn't have his hand around me," I protested.

"Ah, c'mon, Anna, don't mug me off here."

"Seriously, Will. I don't remember him having his arm round me. It's not like that. I barely know him."

"It's what I saw!" Will shouted. Then he turned suddenly and punched the brick wall behind me. A sickening thud. He clasped his hand and groaned. "See what you made me do."

"Will," I yelled, grabbing his arm. "Show me. Are you bleeding?"

He held it up in the poor light. White skin and torn knuckles, blazing red. They looked a little swollen and sore. "You should get that checked."

"I'm fine," he said, flexing it slowly. "See? Now we're both damaged."

"Why did you do it? You could've broken your fist."

"It's you, you drive me crazy. Today I wanted to slash my arms."

"Why . . . ?" My words trailed off.

"I just wanted to get the rage out, you know. It's like it's burning me up. I wanted to hurt myself, to take away what you were doing to me."

"Don't say that. Don't ever say that." The tears were running down my face. How could he think stuff like that? Had I really done this to him?

"Everyone lets me down in the end," he said, his voice soft, almost lost in the breeze.

I pulled him towards me, burying my head in his thick jacket. Breathing in the smell of leather, of aftershave, of him. His arms laced back round me, hugged me tight. We were safe again. We were together.

"I'll never let you down. Never," I said.

"A few things have to change," Will said, softly. "It's the only way things can work between us."

We had moved over to the tyre swings at the park. I was sat squarely in mine, my feet lifted from the ground, gently rocking from side to side. Will sat on the edge, his trainers scuffing the patchy tarmac. "You need to be my girlfriend. Everyone needs to see that. I don't want to be messed around."

"But I'm not messing anyone around."

"That's cool." He smiled at me. "Then you won't mind not meeting up with the lads from the estate. I don't want people seeing you, thinking you're with one of them. I don't want it winding me up. It's not fair."

"That's crazy. . ." I started to protest, but I saw something shift in Will's eyes.

"I thought you'd do that for me."

There was part of me that wanted to argue, tell him he was making a big deal about nothing. But on the other hand, was this really such a big ask? I was hardly mates with any of those guys. It wouldn't be such a big loss.

"Fine," I said. I even forced out a smile. *See, this is easy*.

"I knew you'd be cool. You understand, that's what makes you so special," he said, grinning.

"Of course I'm cool. I just want you to trust me."

"Also. . ." He let the word hang between us for a few seconds, almost teasing. "I want to see more of you."

"I'll try," I said. "Whenever I can, I'll be with you."

He leant forward a little, nearer to me. I kept looking up at his face. Even in the darkness, you could still see how handsome he was. Cute hair. Soft smile. And those eyes, jeez. . . He kept talking, obviously not put off by my soppy staring.

"Like right now, here in this place. This is good. Just us, right now." His eyes gazed around, at the looming shapes of the playground equipment, the eerie glow from the slide. "This should be our time."

I stopped rocking. I stopped staring. "Will, you know that's hard for me. If Dad's working, I have to look after Eddie. And if Dad's home, he'd never let me out. Never mind being grounded, he wouldn't let me out this late."

Will sighed. "If you loved me, you'd do whatever it took. I know I would."

"That's not fair." My voice was sounding like a whine now. I hated myself for it. What was I going to do next? Stamp my feet?

"Why are you letting your dad rule you like this anyway? This is your life. Your chance to get it right."

"I know, but. . ."

"But nothing!" Will got up and strode over to

the roundabout. He gave it a shove. "I can't believe you're letting *him* get between us. This is what he wants. He probably doesn't approve of me."

"Why wouldn't he approve?"

Even in the darkness I could see the glint of his eye. "You know why, Anna. Don't act dumb."

I shook my head. "He knows nothing about you. Anyway, he's not like that."

Because he wasn't. Yeah, OK, a blond-haired, blue-eyed posh boy might irritate him a bit. Dad might make a few judgements. But if he did, he'd keep them to himself.

"Dad doesn't like me dating someone older. And he doesn't like me lying to him."

I felt sad suddenly. Dad had always said how much he hated liars. He saw them as cowards, the lowest of the low. And then Mum started doing it to him, hiding stuff from him, sneaking about behind his back. Quickly followed by me.

"If he gave you more freedom, you wouldn't need to lie. You're not Eddie's mum."

I flinched. I didn't need reminding.

"And anyway, I'm sure you could slip away." Will paused. "Do they even notice you're gone?"

It was like he'd punched me. My whole body

stiffened. I wanted to shout back, to tell him he was out of order, but of course he wasn't. "I don't think they know I'm there most days," I whispered. "I hate that the most. It's like I'm not me any more."

Will took both my hands in his. "Do you see? Can't you understand what's going on here? *We're* good. We could be the best thing ever, but we're letting other people screw this up for us. We need to take control. Just us. That's all we need."

"Yes. . ." I said, squeezing his hands, feeling his warmth.

"Promise me. Promise me you'll do things my way now. I swear it's for the best."

"Promise," I whispered.

From somewhere not far away, I could hear a car alarm going off, screeching into the night. The wind was swirling a little, rustling the few trees that surrounded us. Over the back of the houses, a man shouted, his voice distorted and hollow.

Other than that, other than those disjointed sounds, it could've just been us in the whole world.

I've sorted out lots of stuff, things that basically needed to be cleared up ages ago.

I also told Mum she's a loon. Yep, a proper freak. I told her I hate her for everything she's done to me. I hate the fact that I remind her of you. I can't help it that I look like you. I wish I didn't. I wish I looked like anything BUT you.

I shouted at her. I asked if she even knew why you'd left. What actually happened that night. But she just told me to go away, to "shut my mouth". She knows what happened, but she'd never tell me. Maybe it makes it more real. Talking, I mean.

I told her I wished it was her, not you, who had gone.

She went to hit me.

Can you believe it? With her stick of a hand, that wouldn't even leave a mark. She would've snapped in two. I laughed and left her crying.

I've had enough. I need to get out.

I can't end up a nutjob like her.

I knew it wouldn't take long for my form teacher, Ms Harris, to want to talk to me. Will warned me that they'd be "on my case" within a few days. I smiled when she gestured for me to wait back. I knew exactly what was coming.

"Anna, I hope you don't mind me wanting a little chat," she said, softly. "I've been informed that you stopped your counselling sessions."

I smiled up at her large, round face, at her full lips and wild hair that she wore big and proud. "That's right," I said.

"It seemed quite sudden."

"I just don't need it any more," I said. "I don't have to do it, do I?"

"No, of course not." Ms Harris was fiddling with her pen, twisting it between her long fingers.

"Can I go, then?"

"You seem keen to get to lesson."

"I'm always keen, miss." I beamed at her, the sarcasm stinging my tongue.

"Can I just ask – are things OK now? You were struggling when your mum first left. It can be very hard, especially for girls."

I maintained my neutral face. Will told me not to give emotions away, told me it was how people got into your head. They liked to think they understood you.

"It's all cool," I said, smoothly. "Dad is managing everything. It's fine."

She nodded, her hair bouncing lightly. "And I see you're dating Will Bennett?"

This caught me by surprise. I shuffled in my seat. "I – well, how did you know?"

"Anna, honestly, it's hot gossip. I think everyone in the school knows." She leant in slightly. "And he's a lovely lad, but if you ever want to talk. You know . . . I'm here."

"Talk? Why would I want to talk?"

She put the pen down, ran a long finger across the page of the book in front of her. "Oh – I don't know, relationships can be complicated, can't they? Sometimes it's nice to know that you have people to chat to. If you need to, especially now you've stopped the counselling."

I looked at her, confused, really not sure what she was saying. "OK. Thanks, I think."

"And your friends, of course. Maybe you should talk to Izzy? You two were really good friends. Now I see you in form group and. . ."

Suddenly the penny dropped. I jumped up. "This is about her, isn't it? She's been saying something?"

"Well, no . . . not exactly." I could tell she was getting flustered. "I was worried about her, actually. She's seemed a little low lately. And when we spoke, she talked about you a little. . ."

"And said what?" My voice was too loud, but I didn't care.

"She just said you were blocking her out. You seemed to be with Will a lot. And Anna—"

"No!" I picked up my bag. My hands were shaking. "I'm sorry, miss. I appreciate you trying to help, but there really isn't a problem."

"OK, if you're sure. . ."

"I am!" I said, storming out of the door.

In my rush to get away, I nearly knocked some kid flying. I sprang back, apologies flowing from my mouth. It took a second before I realized it was Dan.

He'd stepped back and was glaring at me. His arm was in a sling. His other hand clasped it protectively.

"I'm so sorry, did I. . ." The words were lost.

"It's fine. I'm on my way to get the dressing changed. It's come loose."

"Is it your hand?"

"My wrist. They broke my wrist." His face was pale. I could see a faded bruise around his eye.

"Who did it? Who would do a thing like that?"

Dan flinched away from me. "It doesn't matter," he hissed, before marching off in the other direction. As I watched him walk away, all I could think was how dull his eyes had looked. The twinkle was totally gone.

I had got used to sitting alone in my lessons. OK, so Izzy was next to me in most of them. But she might as well not have been there. It was like sitting next to a stone statue that just grunted and sighed every now and then. But this time was different. This time she was acting odd.

I could tell something was up as soon as I sat down. She was kind of shifting in her seat and making little coughing noises. Eventually she nudged me gently on my arm.

"Anna, I'm sorry for freezing you out," she whispered. "I feel bad."

I smiled. This was better than I'd expected. I guess I felt a bit smug too. She'd been in the wrong. At least she could see it now.

"Can we be mates again?" she asked.

"Course." I flapped my hand like it all didn't matter. "I'd love that."

"I shouldn't have said those things," Izzy said softly, her eyes fixed to the front so Mr Jones didn't notice us talking. "I guess I never realized how serious you and Will were."

"Well . . . we are."

"That's good." I noticed her bite her lip and wondered if she was nervous. It was crazy. We'd been friends for ever. Why would she feel like that?

"He's really cool, honestly, Iz – you just have to get to know him."

Izzy kept smiling, but her face was still facing front. "You can tell me all about it. I really want to hear. Maybe we can arrange a catch-up?"

"Sure. That'll be good." I felt a surge of warmth. I couldn't believe how much I'd missed our chats. It had only been a few weeks, but it felt longer somehow. "Hey, how about we meet up today? Lunchtime?"

Izzy turned. Her eyes narrowed slightly. "Really? Don't you always see Will, then?"

I shrugged. "He won't mind. I'll just text him now."

She watched as I tapped out the message, a small smile still resting on her lips. "You know, I never thought you'd choose me over him," she said.

"He loves me," I whispered. "There's some stuff that winds him up, but I'm sure this will be fine."

Even so, there was a small knot in my stomach as I pressed send. I watched the screen for a few minutes.

He didn't reply.

In fact, I didn't see him for the rest of the day. It was like he'd disappeared.

I went straight home. I was upset that I'd not heard from Will all day. He wouldn't even answer my calls. My mind was starting to overthink, wondering what I might have done to annoy him. It was so confusing.

Eddie had a tummy ache. He was laid out on the sofa feeling sorry for himself and acting a bit pathetic. Even his favourite cheesy pasta wasn't working. “I don’t want to eat,” he grumbled. “I feel sick. I think I’m getting flu or something.”

I flopped down on the sofa next to him. “What’s up?”

“Nothing. I just feel sick. When’s Dad back?”

“You know – just after ten. It’s always the same.”

Eddie’s bottom lip was jutting out, his total sulking face. Most of the time it really annoyed me, but today I felt a bit sorry for him. He did seem more floppy and fed up than usual.

“We can watch something together, something to cheer you up?” I said, nudging him. He nodded back. A trace of a smile.

I flicked through the channels, trying to find something that we might enjoy. Finally I settled on some reality TV show. It was a bit lame, but Eddie seemed to brighten up when a pretty girl came on the screen.

“She looks fake,” I muttered, staring at her skinny, bronzed body. Her lovely, long, glossy blonde hair.

“Nah, she’s hot,” Eddie giggled.

I kept staring at her, wondering if she was the type Will liked. She was thin in that willowy, graceful way. I glanced down at my own stupid body, wrapped up in cheap, shapeless clothes. No wonder Will was on at me all the time, wanting me to take better care of myself. I was a mess. I needed to look like her. She was the type that boys lusted after. Perfect.

Just thinking about Will was stressing me out. I'd checked my phone at least a hundred times since getting home and he still hadn't got back to me. Was he really annoyed? Next to me, Eddie sighed and snuggled into the cushions. I was just about to lie down next to him when there was a knock on the door.

We both shot up. Eddie's eyes looked wild. We always panicked when someone came to the door. We could never forget the debt collectors standing there, shadows in the dark, waiting for cash we never had. Even though they hadn't visited for some time, the memories lingered like a stale scent.

There was another knock, but softer this time. Much softer. My heart settled.

"It's OK," I said to Eddie. "Just wait there."

I knew as soon as I opened the door that it would be Will. He smiled lazily as he leant against the frame. "I just thought I'd pop by," he said, eyes gleaming.

"Seriously?" I was grinning, but inside my blood

was pumping. "You know you shouldn't come here. Dad will. . ."

"Dad will what?" He bent down and kissed me. "I have the right to see you. You're my girlfriend."

"I know." I pulled the door gently against me, hoping Eddie wasn't listening. "I am glad to see you though. I was worried."

Will gently traced his finger down my face. It made me tingle. He trailed it all the way down, until it came to rest at the centre of my neck. He pressed a little. It made me gasp. I felt like he had tightened a tie around my neck. "You shouldn't let me down like you did today. I get so disappointed. I wanted to see you."

I shifted and his finger dropped. I could still feel the pressure there. "You're freaking me out," I said.

"Freaking you out?" Will's face softened. "I'm sorry, babe, I didn't mean that. I just hated not seeing you at lunch, that's all."

"I'm sorry. Something came up."

"Yeah." He stepped back. "You were with Izzy."

"You saw me?"

"You were seen," he said. "So I guess you two have made up now?"

"Kind of."

He nodded.

"Izzy's lovely, Will. She's my best mate."

"As long as she doesn't get between us?"

"That will never happen."

He was looking at his feet, kind of scuffing them along the floor. But when he looked up, he was smiling again, that bright, beautiful grin that I loved so much.

"Great. Well, everything's cool, then." He moved towards me and pulled me into a hug. His hands stroked my back, worked their way round my waist. "I can't help it. It's you. I don't get why you do this to me. I just want to see you all the time."

"I love you," I whispered into his ear.

He squeezed me tighter and then released me. He was sparkling again. I was forgiven. "Tomorrow night, you come out to see me. We need our time together."

"I—"

"It's either that or I come here. . ."

I thought of Eddie, and then of Dad catching us, and cringed. "No. It's fine. I'll sneak out once Eddie is in bed."

"You are so amazing, Anna," he said. He kissed

me again and then stroked my cheek. "Sometimes I forget myself how special you are."

He turned and walked away, leaving me wanting more, but also leaving me scared at how much I needed him. I was aching all over.

Closing the door, I returned to Eddie, who was curled up asleep on the sofa. Sweaty and cute, like an oversized hamster. Not such a bad kid, especially when he was quiet. I lay down next to him, drinking in his warmth.

Closing my eyes, all I could think of was Will.

BAM! It's hit me. I mean really hit me – what this girl is doing to me.

Is it right that the girl I care about can make me feel like this? I get so wound up when she drops me like I'm NOTHING. Worthless or something. It's not right. I should mean more to her than that.

I should come before everything – right?

I can feel the rage again. It builds up real slow, but it's there, OK.

Rage.

What is it anyway? No one really knows how to control it. They tell you to take deep breaths, count to ten, thump a cushion – but that doesn't get rid of it, does it? It's like chopping down the branches of a tree to try and stop it growing. The trunk is still there. More branches grow in time. Nothing changes.

Sometimes, I just want her to feel my pain. Like I feel the pain every time she upsets me.

You only hurt the one you love.

Right?

Right?

The following day, I did as Will asked. Slipping out of the flat was easy enough. Eddie was always flaked out lately and wasn't making as much fuss about going to bed. It was almost as though he was listening to me for once.

I planned my routine carefully, making sure Eddie had eaten and gone to bed, before I crept away and met Will outside. The park became our new place. Our new shadowy hang-out. Luckily no one else seemed to bother going at that time of night.

"This is just what I wanted," Will murmured, stroking my hair. "Just us two, like it should be. This is what we have to do."

So I carried on. The only struggle was making sure I was home before Dad. Each time I climbed the stairs, my heart would hammer in my chest. I was so scared he'd be home already, but he never was. I could easily get washed and into bed before his footsteps thundered through the flat.

Once or twice, I wound Will up by being late. It was never my fault. It was usually Eddie needing something or taking his time to go to bed. If I was even a minute behind, Will would text me, asking where I was. One time, after Eddie had been feeling ill and delayed me by ten minutes, I ran to the park to find Will waiting by the gate, his eyes ablaze, demanding to know where I had been. I'm not sure he really believed me when I told him. The whole evening he had a sulky expression and blamed me for spoiling everything.

But the following day, Eddie was coughing really badly and needed medicine. When I touched his head, it glowed hot under my palm. I felt awful leaving him, so I stayed an extra fifteen minutes, waiting until his eyelids fell. I felt sick at myself as I crept out of the door.

Even though I was late, I couldn't face the lift. I just couldn't. My hand hovered over the button, but I felt sick at the thought. The last time had been bad enough; I couldn't go through it again. So instead I tore down the stairs, almost tripping on the chipped concrete steps.

Will was waiting just outside of the park. He threw his hands up when he saw me. I could tell he was majorly stressed. "I was just about to leave," he hissed.

"I'm sorry. I had to sort Eddie out. His throat was hurting. I think he's really ill, flu or something."

"I swear you care more about him than me." Will's expression was heavy and dark.

"That's not fair."

"It's not fair making me wait."

"I didn't mean to, I needed to be with him. . ."

"What about me?" he yelled. Then he grabbed my arm hard and pushed me against the fence. "You're making me look like an idiot. You keep doing this. Are you trying to wind me up? Do you enjoy this?"

I couldn't move; he still had a grip of my arm and it was starting to hurt. "Will, can you let go, please?"

He leant in towards me; I could smell his breath, cold and minty. He raised an eyebrow. His eyes were twinkling at me – but they were hard, unkind. "Am I hurting?"

"Yes. . ." I breathed.

He pinched tighter and pushed me further. I could feel the chain fencing biting at my back, catching in my hair. "You're so pathetic. . ." he hissed. "You make me feel sick. Why am I even bothering?"

"Please, Will. I'm sorry. Let me go."

His grip was killing now, burning at my skin. He reached up with his free hand and grabbed a handful of hair. "Look at this! Why have you got your hair like this? It's ugly."

I cringed. I had totally forgotten to brush my hair out of its ponytail. "I'm sorry."

"You're sorry, are you? So, what are you sorry for?"

"I . . . for my hair? For being with Eddie?" I gasped. I used my free hand to reach up to him, try to stroke his face. Make him see I meant it. I wanted to make it better again. I hated it that I'd caused this. That I'd made him angry again.

He tugged my hair, hard. "You look like a slag!" he hissed, before tearing his hand away. Looking down, I could see loose strands in his fingers. I don't know what was burning more, my arm or my scalp, but I was starting to feel really sick. Everything was shifting and hurting slightly. I bit my lip hard and kicked back against the fence. "Please. . ." I whispered.

"Can't you even get that right? You don't even

know what you did wrong," he hissed. "Jeez, you're so thick." Spit was flying from his mouth and landing on my face. "I don't even know why I bother with you, you're just a baby."

He let go then and I staggered further into the fence, like a rabbit in its trap. I kept staring at his dark, angry face. I wasn't even sure who I was looking at any more.

"Go home," he spat. "I'm done with you."

"I'm sorry," I said, tears breaking through the pain. "I didn't mean to make you mad. I just wanted to do the right thing."

"You let me down," Will said coldly. "That's never the right thing. You don't do that to me."

Then he strode away, leaving me sobbing in the dark.

A pathetic, broken mess.

A baby.

I didn't go back to the flat straight away. I stayed, leant up against the stiff chain-link fencing, watching the shadows drift and dance in front of me, praying that Will would return. I just wanted him to sweep me into a hug and tell me that he wasn't angry with me, that it was a crazy joke. Moving also meant it became more real somehow. It wasn't some stupid dream. This had actually happened. I'd upset him. We'd argued. But surely he'd come back to make up. I'd make him see how sorry I was.

But he didn't.

I moved away slowly, legs like jelly and head still throbbing where he'd pulled at my hair. Everything was all jumbled up inside me. I kept reliving the argument, wondering what I could have said differently. Why did I always manage to let him down? Was I such a bad person? I felt like his disappointment was coating me, colouring me in a dirty grey shade. I was nothing. I was a waste. I wasn't worth being with. The pain in my head was a reminder, proof that I'd failed as a girlfriend. I deserved this.

As I turned down the main street towards the towers, the street lights caught in my eyes, making me blink hard. Sharp bubbles of white danced in my vision. I walked almost blindly, just wanting to be back in the towers. Just wanting to hide away and forget everything.

"Anna!"

The shout came from behind me. I turned, hopeful and sick with worry. Was it Will? The figure moved from the corner of the road and I knew instantly that it wasn't. It was Lyn. I felt myself slump slightly. I didn't want to see him. There was no one else I wanted to see right now.

"Hey, Anna!" He strode over towards me, casual as always. "Why are you out here? Bit late, isn't it?"

"What are you? My minder?" I snapped. I kept my head low and my pace fast, hoping he'd leave me alone.

He stopped in his tracks, held out both hands. "Whoa! Don't bite my head off. I was just checking. That's all."

"I'm fine."

I carried on walking. I didn't want Lyn with me. Will had asked me to stay away and I didn't want the grief of him finding out. Because somehow he *would* find out. He always seemed to.

"You don't look fine. You look stressed," Lyn said, walking slightly behind me.

"Seriously, Lyn. It's nothing. Don't worry."

"It's your boyfriend, isn't it? I walked past him about ten minutes ago and he looked like he could murder someone."

I didn't answer. I wished I could shove him away. Why was he bugging me?

"I think I remember where I know his name now," Lyn said softly. "It came to me the other day."

I stopped; I couldn't help myself. "What? What is it?"

Lyn was shaking his head softly. "Well – in truth, it's old stuff . . . you know, rumours and that."

"I'm not interested in rumours." I started walking again; my whole body was shaking. I hated this, the way the Mac was – little whispered tunnels, nudges and glances. No one trusted anyone. It was so pathetic.

"I'm just worried about what you're getting mixed up with."

"Will is cool," I said, feeling my defences going up. I could picture Will in my head now – upset, angry, stressed at me for getting it wrong. Poor Will. I already knew he had to deal with his mum kicking off all the time. No wonder he got wound up sometimes. It was up to me to support him, not make things worse.

I didn't want to talk about him any more. Doing it was tearing at me, feeling like a betrayal.

"Sweet. If that's the case, I'm pleased for you," Lyn said smoothly.

We were marching in silence now, the towers

looming ahead of us. I looked up to my floor, imagined I could see the bright light burning. My home.

"You're lucky, you know. Your dad is so cool," Lyn said suddenly. "A good bloke. I see him around a lot. Everyone likes him here – he seems real and honest."

I felt a sparkle of pride. "Yeah, he's cool, most of the time. Some days he does my head in."

"I used to think that about my dad. But not now." Lyn's voice drifted off. "Family is important, isn't it. . ."

We didn't move for a minute, both of us staring up at the yellow warmth coming from the various windows of the tower. A huge, ugly candle, flickering for us.

"Did you hurt Dan?" I asked quickly, the words tumbling out. "I have to know, Lyn. Was it you?"

Lyn was confused. "Dan? Dan who?"

"Dan Mason who goes to my school. Apparently he upset some kids on the estate. The rumour is they beat him up. I thought it might have been . . . I don't know. . ." My words trailed off. I felt silly asking. "I thought maybe you'd know something at least."

Lyn shook his head. He seemed unfazed, almost

bored. “Nah, sorry. Never heard of him. To be honest, fighting’s not my thing now, you know. . .”

“Yeah, I know.”

He patted my shoulder. “Sounds like you need answers though?”

I nodded. Too many.

That was the problem.

She deserved it. She deserved everything I said to her.

It's weird, that feeling, having her there, begging me to stop – and I couldn't. I was so angry. I couldn't stop. Am I bad? Am I a bad person?

You'd understand, wouldn't you? You'd get it.

You know what it's like to rip your fingernails down someone's skin until they bleed.

You know what it's like to stab at them. To kick them. To bruise them.

You know what it's like. And I remember the look in your eye when you used to do it.

The fun you got from making me cry.

I heard his sobbing as soon as I woke up, shaky and soft. The noise drifted into my room like some kind of sick lullaby. My stomach jolted and I bounced out of bed and ran straight to Eddie.

He was on top of his bed, his covers thrown on the floor. He was a hot sticky mess and his mouth was open in a constant wail. I knelt beside him, gently stroking his damp cheek. "Ed, you OK? I'm here. I'll wake up Dad."

His eyes flickered up and rested on my face. "I couldn't sleep. I ache all over," he moaned.

"I'll get you some water," I said.

"I couldn't sleep," he repeated. "You left me last night. I was on my own."

My body was being twisted. I could feel myself shake. "I wasn't out long," I whispered. "I was back before Dad got home."

"But I was on my own!" His eyes looked so wide and scared. "I called for you and you never came. I thought you'd gone – like Mum. I couldn't sleep after that, I couldn't. . ."

The tears were rolling freely down his sweaty face. The guilt was gnawing at me, telling me what a terrible sister I'd been. Why was I getting everything wrong?

I grabbed his hand and squeezed it tight. "I won't leave you at night again," I said.

"Promise?"

"Promise."

I thought of Will, but quickly forced the worry away. I didn't even know if he wanted to see me again, and if he did, I'd have to figure something out.

"I miss Mum," Eddie whispered, his eyes blinking hard. "When I was ill, she'd sit with me. She'd tell me stupid made-up stories."

I smiled. "She did that for me too."

"Do you miss her?"

I hesitated. The usual words were there in my mouth. I wanted to say "no" and "I hate her" and "I never want to see her again". But I looked carefully at Eddie's sweet, open face and saw similar pain reflected back at me. We were the same.

"I miss her every day," I whispered, almost choking.

"I want to see her. But I want you there too," Eddie said.

"You want me? Seriously?"

Eddie looked at me, his eyes wide. "Yeah. Of course. You're my sis, ain't you?"

I nodded. "Yeah, I'm your sis all right."

I squeezed his hand again, letting the tears flow. Eddie closed his eyes. He seemed calmer now. "Anna?" he said, his eyes still shut.

"Yeah?"

"One day can you do me eggs like Mum used to?"

I sniffed, confused. "What, scrambled?"

"Yeah, like that . . . I love them. She did them the best way."

"I'll try," I said. He smiled. I got up slowly, wanting to let him to rest. "I'll get you some medicine," I whispered.

As I turned, I saw Dad standing in the doorway.

He was watching both of us, silently weeping.

I didn't want to go to school at all, but I knew I couldn't miss any more days. They would start hassling Dad and that was the last thing I wanted.

The ride was weird. I was completely zoned out, watching as the cars passed by and other people wandered along – caught up in their own lives. My thoughts kept switching between Eddie and Will. It had been so long since I'd felt such, well, affection for Eddie. Lately all he'd done was irritate me.

Had I just missed that he was feeling pretty rubbish too? It was his way of acting up. By pushing each other away, we didn't have to admit how much we were hurting. What good had that been doing?

I pressed my head up against the glass, feeling the gentle vibration. Closing my eyes, I could picture Mum. I allowed her to sweep herself into my mind, rather than fighting to push her back into the darkness of my memories. I could clearly see her smiling face, her long hair, knotted into a bun, tiny bits slivering out in front of her eyes. Beautiful eyes that seemed to change colour in the light – brown, hazel, green. I remember when she left, how she squeezed my hand tight and begged me to forgive her, and how I'd slapped her away, told her to get lost...

And die.

Hadn't I told her that too?

Was that what I wanted? Really? Never to see her again?

I could imagine standing next to her. Nudging her gently like I used to. Begging her for advice. *What would you do, Mum? Why can't I make my boyfriend happy? Why does everything feel right and wrong at the same time?* If I concentrated hard, I could picture her screwing her face up, like she did when she was really thinking about something. She would speak softly, carefully, taking her time with the answers. She always knew what to say. Her words would be gentle. They would soothe and make everything better.

I opened my eyes, damp now. Emptiness inside. Nothing was clearer. I wished I had Debs to speak to, but I knew that would make Will even angrier. He said he was there for that sort of thing, but I didn't want to bore him with all my problems. He'd think I was pathetic, a whiner. He coped with his mum being ill. He'd expect the same of me, surely?

Why was everything so complicated?

I got off the bus, confused and tired. Everyone was pushing to get out at the same time, so I hung back a bit, taking in deep breaths, trying to stay calm.

As soon as I stepped off the bus, the bright

morning light caught me, making me blink hard. I turned quickly against it and saw him. Will. He was sat on one of the seats, his school bag between his legs, a soft smile on his lips.

"Hey," he said, standing up. "You OK?"

I shuffled awkwardly, not sure what to say. I'd not heard a word from him all night. I'd assumed he was still mad at me. But he looked cool and relaxed. In fact he looked really pleased to see me.

"Hey," I said finally. "What you doing here?"

"I thought it'd be nice to meet you," he said. "Don't I get a kiss?"

"Sure." I walked over and kissed him lightly on the cheek.

Will backed away a bit. "No, not like that. A proper one." He pulled me towards him and his lips were on mine before I could say anything more. It was a good kiss, nice and gentle. And as he moved away he stroked my face tenderly. "Your hair looks beautiful."

I was wearing it down, just as he liked it. I was paranoid it was greasy at the ends, but knew if I'd slicked it up, he would've been upset with me.

"I look awful," I said. "I barely slept."

I wanted to say that it was because of him.

Because I didn't know what the hell was going on any more. But Will was so chilled right then, I didn't want to bring his mood back down. I didn't want to make things bad again.

"You look beautiful." He was still stroking my face, circling my lips. "I love it when you don't wear loads of make-up. Natural is so much better."

I flinched. Did I normally wear too much, then? Was I getting that wrong too?

He took my hand and we started walking towards school. "About last night. . ." he said finally.

"Yeah?" Fear was twisting me inside and out. I had no idea where this was going to go.

"You were wrong. Leaving me hanging like that. But you apologized. So we can forget about it, yeah? Move on?" His words came out quick, tumbling towards me. It took me a while to absorb them.

"I'm sorry," I said. I took a breath. "But you hurt me, Will."

Will snorted and squeezed my hand. "Oh, don't be a drama queen, Anna. I barely did anything. We had a row, that's all. It's normal. That's what people do. You can't be all innocent here; you could see I was upset. You knew I would be. It's like you enjoy winding me up or something."

"But Eddie was ill. . ."

"But he would've been fine for a few minutes. That's all I wanted. It's not much to ask." Will's voice was breaking. He looked really upset.

"OK." I nodded. "But tonight I can't leave him on his own, it's not fair. He needs me too."

Will sighed. "But I want to see you. It drives me crazy that I'm second best all the time."

We were nearing the school gates now. I knew Will was getting stressed. I could tell from his body, the way he was moving. I didn't want that. Not again. My mind was starting to race. "I could see you after school," I said. An idea quickly developed. There was still so much I didn't know about Will. Could this be my chance to dig a little deeper? "Why don't I come back to yours? I'll tell Dad I'm at homework club? That'll give us a few hours. I'll just get the bus back."

"Or we can go the Swamp instead?" Will said, his voice hopeful.

"Nah. I'm sick of that place. I'd rather see your house. You said you wanted me to go, didn't you?" I paused. "That is, if you're not ashamed of me."

"No." Will shook his head, turned away from me. "No, I'm not ashamed of you."

"So?" I was teasing slightly now, widening my eyes. But Will was still not facing me – I could feel a sudden coolness whipping round me.

"Let's leave it, yeah," he said. "Just for tonight. We need to sort it properly. . ."

"But. . ."

"I said leave it," he hissed, facing me again – eyes slitty and hard.

So I did. The coldness inside me was a solid heavy lump. I couldn't swallow. I couldn't speak.

We walked the rest of the way in silence.

Dan was outside English when the lunch bell rang. He was standing there as I came out of my lesson, leaning against the wall, fiddling with his phone. He looked up when he saw me and then quickly went back to his phone again.

"Hey," I said, awkwardly. "What are you doing here?"

"I'm waiting for Miss Elliott," he muttered. "Struggling with my written assignments at the mo, so I need to keep borrowing a laptop."

"How is it?" I asked, still hating to see his hand like that.

Dan just shrugged. "No better."

"Hopefully it won't take too long to heal." I found myself staring at the floor. What else could I say?

"Where you off to, then?" he asked. "Canteen?"

"I'll grab something, then go sit with Will."

"Course," he sighed, a trace of sarcasm there. I prickled a bit at this. I went to say something, but quickly caught myself. It wasn't worth the hassle. Instead I adjusted the strap on my bag and started to move away. "Don't you miss it, Anna?" he said suddenly.

"What?"

"The singing? The band? It's driving me crazy not doing it."

"Aren't you guys still meeting up?" I said.

"What? With no singer and a guitarist that can't play. . ." He made a noise, a half laugh. "The band just isn't happening right now."

I shook my head. I hated that. The band was everything to Dan. It had been everything to me once, too. It wasn't right. They should still be playing.

"Don't you miss it?" he repeated, his voice firmer this time.

I couldn't answer, not straight away. Everything had been so crazy lately, I'd barely had time to think about missing it or not. But that buzzing pressure, those stressful thoughts I had about Mum, about Will, still burned inside me like fire. Singing helped; it always helped. And now I wasn't doing it, the pressure had nowhere to go. It was bubbling away, looking for somewhere to escape.

I stared blankly at Dan, remembering the energy between us. The wonderful vibe, the swell of the music that would sweep us up into a wave of excitement and near hysteria. Of course I missed it. I was feeling so dull now, like a tree with no sunlight. I could almost feel myself fading.

But I had to make sacrifices, didn't I? It was only a silly band. A bit of fun? Sometimes you have to let things go, even if you love them.

"I don't have much time. . ." I whispered.

"You should make time," he said, his teeth gritted. "You're too good to throw it all away."

"I'm not throwing it all away!"

"Fine. . ." He turned away. "If that's what you really believe."

"What choice did I have?" I said, finally snapping. "You never had me in the band for my voice. I know what you really thought of me!"

Dan's cheeks were red now. "What I thought

of you? So, what did I think of you, Anna?" He was almost shouting now. "That you were an amazing singer. That you blew me away. That you were my best mate?"

"Nah!" I moved closer. The embers were lit up inside me. I wasn't stopping now. "You sent that text. I saw it. You said you only wanted me in the band to pull me. You said I was rubbish. . ." My voice broke.

Dan didn't move; his face was frozen. "Text? What text?"

"Don't try and deny it. I saw it. It was from your phone. You sent a text to Callum."

He was shaking his head, a puzzled look on his face. "No way. I didn't. I don't even like Callum that much. He hangs around with knobs like your boyfriend. . ." He was biting his lip. "Man, if I knew this was what was being said, I would've confronted you. I just assumed you were being a tit because of Will."

"I saw it," I repeated, my words shaking.

But Dan was calm now, really calm. "It wasn't me. And if I have to, I'll prove it."

I took a step back, confused now. "You can't prove it, Dan. I wish you'd just admit you said those things about me. Maybe it's true anyway. Maybe I am rubbish."

That's pretty much how I feel...

"You're not rubbish. You're far from it." He groaned suddenly. "Jeez – you left the band over this? You gave up over a pack of lies?"

"I don't know what to believe," I said. Then a new fear grabbed me as I realized how long we'd been talking. "Dan. I have to go. I'll be late for Will."

"You're scared of him, aren't you," he said, reaching towards me. "What is he doing to you? Why does he have such a hold on you? This isn't right."

"I'm not scared of him."

"Whatever." He scowled at me.

"I'm not scared."

His expression changed, softened suddenly. I'd not seen it before. "I wish I believed you... Anna, please, I want you to text me, call me – whatever. Contact me if you're worried about anything. Please don't ever be scared."

"I'm not," I insisted. I smiled brightly as if to prove it. "It's going great, honest."

"You're really not worried about him?"

"No."

"Well. You should be," Dan said softly. "I'm convinced it was Will that did this to me. He set it all up. I think he hates me. He's jealous or something."

Dan pointed to his hand, and although my first reaction was to laugh "Oh yeah, right", there was a scared little voice inside me that wouldn't shut up. "Did you see him?"

"No. They had hoods and scarves over their faces. But I'm pretty sure it's him from what they said."

I'd seen Will's face when it turned dark. I'd seen him change. I'd seen...

"There's something wrong about all this," Dan said. "You've changed. You don't even see Izzy any more. He's controlling you. Can't you see it?"

No, no, no. Not me. I'm lucky. Lucky to have him...

Aren't I?

Aren't I?

"You're worth more than this," he whispered.

"I'm fine," I said. "Honestly."

But I wasn't sure who I was convincing – him or me.

*

By the time I made my way to our spot on the field, Will had gone. I guess I wasn't too surprised. I checked around quickly, but I couldn't see him anywhere.

I had that defeated, flat feeling. Like I'd just lost something really valuable, or offended someone who I didn't mean to. I was so hungry too, having not had a chance to grab any food on the way. It hardly mattered anyway. Despite my growling stomach, I felt too sick to eat.

At least Will would be happy. He hates me eating too much. . .

I stopped myself mid-thought. This felt so wrong. Why was I thinking stuff like this? Had it always been this way? Words from my conversation with Dan kept jumping out at me.

You've changed...

You're scared...

He's controlling you...

This wasn't true, of course. Will loved me. We were cool together. I was so lucky to be with him.

But...

But...

My phone buzzed. I knew who it was before I'd even opened it.

I went out with the lads for lunch. Obvs you're not coming. I'll see you tomorrow then. We'll sort stuff.

I couldn't read his mood. Was he angry? Was he chilled? Why did I even have to stress about it? I bit my lip, feeling the dryness of the skin. Usually I'd stick some lip gloss on or something, try and soften them, but Will hated that stuff.

Controlling you...

My hands flicked up to my hair, frizzy and loose. I'd not had a chance to straighten it this morning and I knew that no serum was going to stop it looking wild. Usually I would have swept it back into a ponytail. But I hadn't today. Because of Will.

Controlling...

He loves you, stupid. Stop doubting it. You wanted this. You still want it. Will Bennett.

But...

But...

Sometimes you have to let things go, even if you love them.

I needed some space. I needed to work stuff out. The thoughts were crowded inside of me. I couldn't even figure out which voice was right.

Fact 1) It was the years spent creeping in your shadows, trying not to upset you, that have totally screwed me up.

Fact 2) I don't need a counsellor to tell me that.

Fact 3) I don't need a counsellor to tell me that a ten-year-old kid shouldn't be hurt. Not just hurt. Beaten. Because you enjoyed that, didn't you?

Fact 4) I don't need a counsellor to tell me that Mum should've stopped you, instead of thinking kicking and punching was just normal, to toughen me up. Play-fighting, she called it. I don't think I was ever laughing. But you were.

Fact 5) I don't need a counsellor to tell me that Mum ignored everything because it was easier that way.

I don't need it.

It's too late now. You've made me like you.

I see what you see.

It's like this with Anna. I can grab her, hurt her. I can do it, because it's easy. I can't help it. My hand flies up. I feel powerful, alive. Right or wrong – this is who I am.

I'm like you.

I don't know how to stop it.

I wasn't expecting to sleep well. At least that was something I got right. For a bit I just lay on the bed, hardly moving, listening to the sounds around our flat. Comforting sounds. Sounds that hadn't ever changed. Dad singing softly along to some naff song on the radio. Eddie chatting to him, obviously feeling better. The sounds of "coping" and "getting on". Somehow we had managed to muddle through the last few months, sticking ourselves back together with our own form of Sellotape. It wasn't a permanent solution. It was shaky, but we were OK.

I'd made my mind up about something, though. I would see Mum again. I had to. I had things to say and only she could hear them. I was ready now.

I walked into the kitchen and Dad smiled at me. Eddie flicked up his finger as usual, but this time I grinned and flicked one back.

"You feel better, then?"

"Yeah . . . I just wanna eat," he said, biting into his toast as if to make the point. "It feels like years since I got some food."

"He's all good," Dad said. "He has the best team looking after him."

I glanced over at Eddie, wondering if he would say anything about me leaving, but he didn't flinch. He just kept on eating. A silent agreement hung between us. He was going to let it go.

I took a shaky breath. Most of the night I'd been thinking, turning stuff over in my mind. The only thing that had become clear was that I didn't want to lie to Dad any more. It wasn't how we worked. Dad had been lied to long enough. We all had.

"I'm going to see Will today," I said softly.

Dad was cleaning the work surface down. He stopped and although I couldn't see his face, I knew he was frowning. I could see the big muscles in his neck tense up. "Are you trying to wind me up?"

"No. I'm trying to be honest."

"Well, that's very noble of you, but I can tell you now – you're not going."

I waited for a minute or two, counting the seconds in my head. I had to get this right. I could see

Eddie was eating slower now, was dead interested in what was going on. The atmosphere was tight, edgy.

"Please, Dad, I need to do this. I don't want to go behind your back. I really don't."

He turned. His face was like stone, but I could see the softness in his eyes, the flicker of worry. "What do you need to do?"

"I need to find out what's going on. I think Will has been upsetting my friends." I thought of Dan's hand and cringed at my blatant understatement. "I just need to talk to him. That's all. I'll be back early. I promise."

I could see he was wavering. His mouth was working slowly, taking time over his answer. "And what if he has been doing this stuff? What then?"

"Then. . ." My stomach was surging. "Then . . . I don't know."

"You really like him, don't you?"

I nodded.

Dad sighed and threw down the dishcloth. "And I'm guessing you'll go there whatever I say."

I nodded again.

"Thought so." He came towards me and gently squeezed my shoulder. I glanced down at his big, bear-like hand. He'd never hurt me, never been too rough or too heavy. He was as gentle as a feather. "Then I guess I have to trust you to do the best thing," he said.

As he walked out the room, I felt a surge of relief. No more lies. I felt part of the tension lift inside of me.

Eddie slammed his glass down. "I just wish you'd dump the loser," he hissed.

"Eddie!" I turned to him, shocked.

"Well – I'm sick of it. He's an idiot."

"Why are you saying that?"

"You don't get it, do you?" Eddie snorted. "He tried getting at me and threatening me. Telling me to stay away from you two or he'd have me hurt." He sniffed. "I don't care any more. I'm not scared of him."

"Eddie! Seriously? Why didn't you say something before?"

"I did! I told Dad, thinking it would end things between you. But you were obviously so into him that it was never going to change. It's not like I was bothered at first. I just thought it was all so pathetic. But then he came right in my face that first night he came over. Told me to keep my distance. Told me not to breathe a word if you left the flat with him."

"Eddie, that's awful." I was struggling to find the right words. "I'm so sorry."

"He's a nutter!" Eddie said, shaking his head. "And you're a nutter for going out with him." He was looking at me like I was a complete loser, his eyes squinted up, his head shaking in mock pity.

Usually I would've told him to get lost. But I couldn't. I just kept staring at his disgusted face, trying to figure out why I hadn't known this stuff before.

As I stood there, slowly the jumbled parts of my mind were moving and coming together. The picture was becoming clearer. So much clearer now.

Will was meeting me at the bus stop. As the bus approached, I tensed up. This was stressful. This wasn't how I imagined things would be.

You just need to talk. It'll be cool. If you have to, you can end this. You can do it.

The bus was rammed again, so I was standing at the front gripping the rail. Behind me a group of girls, probably aged about eleven or so, were laughing over some picture on their phone. "Just look at the state of her . . . she looks minging. . ." I wondered who they were looking at. A month ago, that would've been me and Izzy – laughing together, being silly.

And it will be again. You just need to tell Will straight. He'll respect you for it. He needs to see things for how they are. You need to be clear with him.

And if he doesn't like it, then what?

I shook my head, not wanting to think about that.

The bus shuddered to a stop, nearly flinging me across the aisle. I staggered off, slightly unbalanced. I checked myself as I did so, smoothing down my unruly hair, fixing a smile on my tired face. I had to make this work. I had to prove to everyone that Will was cool, that he wasn't this monster they were making him out to be.

I saw him straight away, leaning against the shelter. He was squinting into the sun, giving him a slightly mean and moody look. He smiled when I came over, and ruffled my hair. "Cute. I like it."

"It's no different," I said.

"It's straighter, isn't it? It looks nice anyway, really pretty."

"I guess." My hand absently touched the loose bits. Did he not like it natural? I was starting to overthink again.

"My house isn't far away," Will said, flapping his hand behind him. "Come on. Let's go."

"Your house. . ." I stuttered. I wasn't expecting this. I'd assumed we were going to the Swamp again. "Why did you change your mind?"

"I wanted to prove I wasn't ashamed of you." Will shrugged. "It's no big deal." His face looked pinched and strange though. I couldn't help thinking this *was* a big deal.

He gripped my hand with his and we started walking. I could feel a slight tension between us, an electricity that hummed tonelessly. My mind was whirring. This wasn't what I was expecting at all.

"I missed you yesterday," he muttered. "What happened?"

"I—" I wanted to tell him. I wanted to be honest, but I felt trapped. "I was held up in my lesson, I'm sorry."

He squeezed my hand. "It's OK. Did you get my messages?"

I nodded. I thought of the numerous texts he'd sent last night, which in the end I'd been too tired to answer. Most of them saying the same thing: *You're mine*, *I love you*. *What you doing?* Reading them, I'd had the usual sensation of happiness, the reassurance that he still wanted me. But something else had niggled at me, an unease. Something that hadn't been there before.

"When we're apart, I keep thinking about you." He half laughed. "It's crazy really. I never thought I'd be like this."

"It's sweet," I said.

"Just don't tell everyone. I probably sound so lame."

I was starting to relax. Will was obviously pleased to see me. This was all good. I could talk to him and he wouldn't kick off. It would be fine.

"I hope you don't think . . . I dunno. . ." He was struggling, his free hand gesturing like it was trying to help him find the words. "I just hope you don't think differently after you see her."

"See who?" I was confused. "Your mum?"

"Yeah . . . her," he sighed. "You might, I dunno – judge me or something."

I tugged on his hand, made him look at me. "Do I look like someone who judges? Seriously?"

"No. . ." He half smiled.

"Good."

He led us round a corner into a side street and

then slowed up. Let go of my hand. "This is it. My place."

I turned to where he was facing. The house didn't look any different to the others on the street – rows of old terraced houses with brown pebble-dashed walls. I don't know what I was expecting – super posh or something? It was big. Certainly nicer than my place, but it wasn't what I'd imagined. The front fence was black metal, chipped in places, leaving grey scars behind. The garden was overgrown with weeds, grass licking at the garden path. Dark curtains shielded the window next to a wooden porch that looked like it had wilted in the rain. It looked a bit neglected, sad and forgotten. In need of love.

"My dad's not around now," Will said. I think he saw me staring.

He strolled up the path, leaving me to trail behind. I could see a cat hiding in the huge shrubs, peering at me with narrow yellow eyes. It hissed and I jolted, uneasiness sweeping through me again.

Will was opening the door. "I'm not sure if she's up," he whispered. "We'll check the living room. If not, don't worry."

I followed him into the musty gloom. The darkness overtook me. Everything seemed dingy and grim. The curtains were heavy, keeping out the light. It was eerie. Not right.

Will pushed open the door on his left and immediately sighed. "Hello, Mum."

I kept close behind, blinking hard. Although it was still dark in there, the smell was clean, almost clinical – artificial, like a heap of air fresheners had been sprayed everywhere. Will stepped aside and I could see the living room properly. It was tidy. Nothing was out of place. Leather sofas were shining against the wallpapered walls; the carpet was soft and fluffy, the wooden furniture gleamed.

And there were pictures everywhere. On the wall. On the mantelpiece. All of a boy with dark hair and laughing eyes.

A boy that clearly wasn't Will.

And there in the corner was a woman sitting in the chair.

Will's mum was not like him at all. She looked like a tiny bird, her legs drawn up under her, and her chin resting on her arm. Short dark hair and pale, pale skin. She was smiling softly as she read something. A book of some sort. Her finger was trailing across the page, up and down – almost like it was stroking the paper.

"Mum?" Will said softly. Like a test.

She looked up. Her eyes seemed out of focus. "Ah." She smiled. "You're home." Then she went back to her book, all interest gone.

"I brought Anna to meet you. My girlfriend?" Will's voice seemed different somehow. Slightly pleading. I looked at his face and I could see his wide eyes, his nervous face. He seemed so small, all the swagger gone.

"Mmmm." She was still reading, her long fingers busy combing the page. They freaked me out, those fingers. Too thin, too white – like brittle bones.

"Anna – this is my mum," Will said, as if I didn't know. He gave me a small shove in my back and I felt obliged to step forward.

"Hi," I said. "It's great to meet you." My voice was shrill and forced.

Her focus drifted up again. I could see the mistiness there, like she wasn't quite connecting. It reminded me of Izzy's nan – how she barely remembered her, even though she visited every week.

"Anna. . ." He voice was soft. "You're not what I was expecting."

I flinched. The spark inside me flickered, but I fought against it. This wasn't the time.

"What are you reading, Mum?" Will asked behind me.

"Oh – this." She flapped at the pages. I could now see it was some kind of exercise book. "It's Jez's. Some of his school work. I like to see his writing. . ."

I looked at Will, confused. Jez?

Will swore behind me and muttered something under his breath. I stood, feeling uncomfortable, feeling the tension grow.

"C'mon on, Anna, let's go upstairs," he said finally.

His mum returned to the book, her finger tracing the letters, her mouth silently sounding out the words, like a child learning to read.

"Leave her," he said, his voice firm now. "She's mental. I told you. It's useless."

As we left the room, Will slammed the door behind him. I jumped at the sound.

"Useless!" he sputtered through gritted teeth.

Will's room was like the living room: clean, tidy, functional. In fact it freaked me out. Like the living room, there wasn't a thing out of place. The bed was made and tucked away under the window. The dressing table had a glass of water on it and a clock – nothing else. There were no posters, no clothes on the floor, nothing.

"Mess freaks her out even more," he said, as if to explain.

I sat on his bed, trying to relax, but Will was obviously worked up. He kept pacing the floor, restless and agitated. "There's always something. She never gives up," he said, clawing his hands through his hair. "She goes on about him all the time."

"Who? Who's Jez?"

Will stopped and turned. His eyes were glinting in rage. "Yeah, yeah. It's always about him. Didn't you see pictures of him everywhere? She's obsessed. She can't let him go."

"Is he. . . ?" I tried to find the right words. "A brother or something?"

"Yeah . . . yeah, my brother. But he left years ago. Ran away. She's never been the same since."

"She does seem a bit. . ."

"Nutty? Yeah, you could say that. I mean she's never been completely normal but Jez walking out just flipped her over. He was up to his eyes in trouble. We had people banging at the door, after him. She got so scared she wouldn't leave the house. It all changed after that."

"What had he done?" I asked gently.

"What hadn't he done? He was a thug. He upset everyone – except her!"

"She loves him, I guess," I whispered.

But Will wasn't listening. "She always forgives him. She thinks she got it wrong, or. . ." He was pacing now. "She zones out totally. Every day is the same, more or less."

"Sorry." I eased myself forward. "But is your dad not around at all?"

"He comes and goes when it suits him. It does his head in, too."

"It must be hard."

"Hard?" He spat the word at me. "It's bloody unbearable. What the hell would you know?"

He was standing inches in front of me. I could see his fists were curled. Everything inside me tightened. I needed to get away. I needed to break the tension.

"I'm sorry. I need the loo, Will," I said quickly. "I'm bursting. Is it out there?"

He blinked, then nodded. I slid past him quickly, noticing how he flopped on the bed as I left.

The small bathroom was no real escape. There was no lock on the door. I shut the toilet lid and sat on it, resting my head on the cool wall. Even in here it was grim. Brown walls, a shower curtain with a tear in it and a shower head that hung loose from its attachment, dripping slowly. Everything felt weary and unloved.

I could leave. I could just go, right now.

But you want to sort this. You have to.

Reaching inside my pocket, I pulled out my phone.

I'm talking to him now, I texted quickly. I'm at his house but he's angry. Can you come? Just in case. Wait outside?

Then I quickly shoved it away before I could change my mind.

Inside my pocket I felt the buzz of the reply.

I sat next to Will on the bed. He looked more relaxed now; his legs were stretched out, his face was calm.

Will started stroking my leg. "I really don't want to talk about Jez or my mum. It just makes me angry. This is our time now. It's precious. We shouldn't waste it on *them*." He said the word "them" like it had left a nasty taste in his mouth.

"I understand."

"I knew you would." His voice was barely a whisper. "That's what's so amazing about you. You get it."

I nodded and let him move towards me. I found my hand touching his face, pulling on his shirt to draw him closer. The kiss was delicious, slow and sweet. I wanted to keep it for ever, but in the background my mind was still working. I pulled away. "But I have to ask something," I said.

Will groaned. "Why stop now? That was so good."

"Will. I have to ask this, I'm sorry. I need to know."

"What?" he sighed. "What is it?"

"Did you hurt Dan? Was it you?" I swallowed hard and inched towards him, taking his hand in mine. "Please, Will, please tell me you didn't do that to him."

And in that split second, everything changed.

You deserved everything that happened to you.

There. I've said.

And I don't miss you. I should. But I don't.

Not really.

I won't cry for you like Mum does.

You deserved everything.

You ruined everything.

I'm nothing because of YOU.

“What the hell is wrong with you? Why won’t you leave things alone?” Will thumped the bed and then jumped up. “You have to keep digging and digging, like a little rat. It’s like you never listen to me.”

“I just want to know the truth,” I said, trying not to shrink back. “You hurt him, didn’t you? And you threatened my brother?”

“So what if I did?” His face was in mine now. Pure rage. “So what? If things need sorting, I sort them. That’s how it is.”

“What needed sorting?” I tried to keep my voice gentle, to calm him, but I could hear the tremor there, betraying me. I was losing this.

“People interfering!” He stepped back and threw his hands in the air. “Jeez, what sort of idiot are you? You think Dan was your mate? He just wanted to score with you. He was making you look like a fool.

As for your brother, spoilt little loser – I told him how it is. He needed telling."

"Dan said he didn't send the text."

"And you believe him?"

I hesitated, bit my lip, then I answered. "Yeah. I believe him."

Will came at me like a raging animal. He grabbed my hair and yanked it back, tipping my whole head up. Heat shot up my neck, into my scalp. It took my breath away. "You believe him over me?" he hissed.

"Yes," I said through gritted teeth, tears piercing through. I wasn't going to lie. Not now.

"Maybe I got this all wrong. Maybe you liked Dan all along?" He pulled harder; his free hand clasped the skin around my neck, pinching it, making it difficult to breathe. "Yeah, I get it now. You were just using me to make him jealous. It explains why you always stick up for him. Who else would bother? Most girls would listen to their boyfriends."

"I don't like Dan. Please, Will. . ." I gasped. The pain was crazy now. Air was rattling through my throat, fighting. I could feel pressure behind my eyes. "I thought we could talk. . ."

"Talk! You're just accusing me!"

"I'm not, please. . ."

He let go suddenly and then shoved me hard, backwards on to the bed. My head hit the wall and I swore. "Will. . ." I ran my hand over my neck. Wanted to cough. To splutter. Everything was on fire.

"Look at you . . . pathetic," he spat. "Why would I want to be seen with you? Why do I bother?"

"I'm sorry I upset you." I tried to sit up, feeling giddy and sore. "I thought we could talk. But maybe not. I really want to go now."

"You really want to go now?" His voice mimicked mine, cruel and mocking. As he reached down, his hand skimmed my breasts. He moved forward, touching them again. I shrank away. "What's the matter? I thought you loved me?" he hissed.

"Not this," I said. "Please, Will. . ."

His eyes glinted again. "Not what? Seriously! Do you think I'd touch you now?" He laughed. "You're nothing but an ugly slag."

Ugly slag. . .

Slag. . .

I hardened. Every slap, pull and pinch had hurt – but this was worse somehow. This pain was sharper, more intense. Immediately I thought of Dad. Of his strong, honest way. Dad would never put up with this. Suddenly I needed him more than ever. How had I got this so wrong?

Will was leaning over me, his cruel, nasty face still leering at me. His true reflection. "I'm going." I pushed him and went to get up.

Will pushed me back. "You're not going anywhere!"

My eyes flared. I wanted to spit at him. "You're letting me go, otherwise I'll scream. . ." I hissed.

Will shrugged, but he backed away a bit. "She wouldn't care anyway. . ." he muttered.

"You touch me again and I'm screaming this whole house down," I said, pulling myself up. I didn't recognize the ice in my voice. "The whole bloody street will hear."

Will laughed. "Just listen to you! Who the hell do you think you are?"

My voice was louder now. "Someone is coming, Will. They will knock on the door. They are coming to check I'm OK."

Will shifted, his cold smile still cutting like ice through me. "Yeah . . . right. . ." His spit sprayed on my face. It was all I could do not to gag.

"They are," I said, calmer now. "I told them to come."

Something changed in his face. Coldness for

disgust. A smile for a sneer. He moved away from me, flapped his hand like I was nothing.

"Go on, then," he said, his voice slow and calm. "Go! You pathetic, frigid bitch. You make me feel sick anyway."

He turned away from me.

He was stone.

I walked out of the room as quickly as my shaky, half-dead legs would take me.

I passed the closed door of the living room, pausing for a split second. I wondered what his mum was doing in there. Had she heard Will shouting? Did she even care? Or was she still pawing over that book of Jez's, lost in her own world, trapped in the past?

I couldn't wait to get out of there. To leave that weird, dark place behind. I tumbled out of the door and on to the street. My feet were so heavy, I was struggling to move them, but I made my way slowly along the path. My throat was still killing – I felt like my windpipe had been doused in acid. I kept swallowing, wishing the pain would go.

All I could do was walk. Walk away, trembling and heavy-legged. I fumbled in my pocket for my phone.

"Anna!"

I looked around blindly. Surely not Will?

Please leave me alone... Just go...

I tried to run, but then my eyes adjusted and I saw him properly. I nearly fell to the ground in relief.

"Anna!" Dan grabbed me roughly, wrapped me in his arms. I wanted to cry but couldn't. Nothing seemed to be working right.

"You came," I said instead.

"Of course I did. As soon as I saw your text." Dan was frowning; he reached towards my face. "Your neck is all red. Jeez, Anna, are they nail marks?"

"I think so."

"He did this to you? You should've got out sooner."

"He got mad so quickly," I said, rubbing my skin, feeling the trails of hurt he'd left there. "He just exploded when I asked about you." I felt too embarrassed to say the rest.

"I'm so sorry..." Dan breathed out hard. "I should've come quicker. If I'd known..."

"There's nothing you could've done to stop him." I touched the skin around my throat again. It felt so tender.

"I would've hammered the door down, got you out of there. He's a bloody psycho." Dan was shaking his head, his face red and mad. "You need to call the police. This is assault. He can't get away with it."

"I'm not doing that." I was so tired. All I wanted to do was sleep. "I just want it to be over. I was so stupid."

The tears started racing from me. I couldn't stop them now. I hated breaking down in front of Dan, but I couldn't stop.

"Should I call my mum or something? Or your dad?"

I shook my head.

"I'll take you home. You probably need to get your head around all this," he sighed. "I knew he was a bit of a nutter, but not this bad. I didn't think he'd hurt you like this."

"It's OK. . ."

"Let's walk to my house at least. I can get you home from there."

I nodded. That sounded good. Dan walked with me, his good hand carefully curled around my back like he was leading me.

"Thank you for coming," I said. "I guess I had a feeling it wasn't going to turn out right. I needed someone to know where I was."

"I'm glad you told me," he said.

"I'm sorry he busted your wrist."

Dan grimaced. "It's fine. Well, it's not, but it's not your fault. I always knew it was him. Him and Callum. It was obvious. They told me to stay away from you. I guess I was a coward, because I did. I didn't want to make things worse."

"You're not the coward."

"I'd heard stuff about his family," said Dan. "I wasn't sure if it was true or not. Maybe I should've warned you. But I didn't think it was my business. And would you have listened anyway?"

I leant against the wall, trying to stop the throbbing in my head. "Why couldn't I see what he was like?"

"I guess you liked him."

I sniffed. "He could be really nice, you know. He made me feel special."

Dan shifted awkwardly. "You *are* special, Anna. You don't need Will to tell you that. You have to listen to other people too."

I could feel myself blush. "Thanks."

"He sent the text too," Dan said gently. "I did what you said. I asked Callum. Apparently they got my phone while I was playing football. Wrote out the text and sent it for Cal to forward to Will." Dan shrugged. "I guess it was quite smart on their part.

Callum just thought it was a big joke, the idiot."

The anger was bubbling again. "I shouldn't have believed him," I whispered.

"No, you shouldn't have," Dan replied softly.

I closed my eyes.

All I could see was Will's face.

All I could hear were those words.

Slag.

Ugly slag.

Frigid bitch.

In my pocket, my phone buzzed loudly. I flinched and my eyes opened. Dan was staring. "Don't look at it," he warned. "Not yet."

But my hand was already pulling it out. I knew it was Will. I guess I was expecting it.

The message was pretty unclear at first.

You shouldn't upset me. Come back now or else this will be going to everyone.

But then I clicked on the attachment. It took a few seconds for my eyes to register the image, but when it did, I wished they were still closed.

The image of me in the Swamp.

In my bra.

*

"We'll sort this, stop panicking," Dan said, trying to calm me. But I was beyond it.

"How could he do this? It's evil," I shouted. I held up my phone, wanting to hurl it against the wall. "You're a freak!" I screamed, as if he could hear me. I wanted to reach inside the screen, to grab his smug face and yell right into it.

I remembered the day at the Swamp. Me paddling in the grimy waters. Will standing behind, watching me. I never knew he'd taken a picture. He'd had his phone out. Why hadn't I realized!

Why?

Why!!!

"We could tell your dad. He'll sort it."

"I'm not telling my dad, Dan." The thought of Dad knowing made me hurt inside.

"I'm sure it's illegal," Dan said. "We should tell *someone*."

"I'm not fighting him," I said. "I'm done with this." The certainty was there. I knew now what I had to do.

I tried to keep calm as I typed out my reply, my fingers like bullets, my hands shaking as they clasped the phone.

Do what you like. I'm not scared.

I wasn't running any more.

Yeah, so what, I get angry.
I'm done talking now.

I barely slept. Another broken night. Salty tears and bitter sobs turning into raging words and angry, twisted thoughts. I turned my phone off, not wanting to see the abuse that had been set up for me. I already knew the entire year group would be swarming at my picture now on the internet somewhere, making comments, passing judgements.

I turned my phone off, not wanting to hear from the one person who had caused all this.

I didn't deserve this.

As I lay back on my bed, watching circles of light dance against my ceiling – things began to stir and settle within me.

If being with Will meant hurt and pain, then he could stick it.

If being with Will meant I was his figure of fun – then I couldn't stand any more.

If being with Will meant I couldn't be me – then where the hell did that leave us?

By morning, I knew the answer.

The looks said it all. Sniggers in the form room. Whispers behind my back. I tried to be prepared, but I wasn't. Not at all. I just wanted to hide.

He did this to me. He humiliated me. It was like the final knife in my back.

Of course I could've missed school. I could've avoided this. I couldn't even bring myself to check online; I didn't want to see it again. I relied on the thin hope that Will had come to his senses and deleted the image. Apologized, maybe?

After all, he loved me. Had loved me. Hadn't he?

Obviously not.

I heard the broken bits of conversation as I moved down the corridor:

"... did you see...?"

"... just bra. So funny."

"... cringe..."

"... seriously, look at her..."

I tried to keep my head high, to remain calm and unbothered. A group of Year Sevens were gathered by the stairs. They looked at me and then burst out laughing. They might as well have pelted me with missiles; I could feel every strike.

Without thinking, I ran into the nearest toilets. I wanted to crawl into the smallest space and hide. I wanted to die. This was me they were talking about, my body, my horrible, stupid body.

I splashed cold water on my face, bursts of sharp icy spray. I couldn't look in the mirror. I didn't want to see my face, the idiot mug that everyone was laughing at.

There was a movement in the toilet behind me. The chain flushed and then Kacey, a girl in my year, stepped out.

"Jeez, Anna," she said. "Your picture is everywhere."

I glared back at her. Did I really need telling?

"Did you know he was going to do it?" she whispered.

"No," I spat back.

"Well . . . maybe you shouldn't have let him take it the first place." Her perfectly plucked eyebrow was raised. "Just saying."

I wanted to scream back, but stopped myself. Why did I have to justify myself to her? Even if I'd let Will take the picture, that didn't give him the right to broadcast it to the world.

"He's in the wrong, not me," I muttered.

So why was it me feeling so bad?

I spent the morning slumped in class, buried in my books, trying to ignore the giggles and whispers around me. The same voice kept echoing though my head:

You've done nothing wrong.

Each time, a bit more of my rage was ignited.

As I walked to my seat in art, I saw Izzy talking with some others. She was giggling, and then quickly her glance fell on me. My heart sank, wondering if she was talking about me too.

She came over and slid on to the seat next to me. Her smile was sweet and sympathetic. "I'm sorry," she said. "What he did. . . That's mean. So low."

"Was that what you were all laughing about?" I said, glaring at her.

"Actually, we were saying what a loser Will was. You can totally tell he sneaked up on you. That's nasty."

"Really? Is everyone saying that?"

"Yeah, most people. You're looking at him all surprised, not posing or anything. It's obvious you didn't know what he was doing. That's pervy if you ask me. Weird."

"Yeah . . . it was a bit odd."

"At least your bra looks nice." She nudged me. "It could be worse."

"Could it?" I felt so miserable, I wanted to fall in her arms and sob.

"You have nothing to be ashamed of. If anything, you should be thankful. You got out." Izzy leant in closer. "I heard he was really nasty to his ex as well and she was with him for months."

I looked back at her, surprised. So it wasn't just me? "He called me a slag," I whispered. "I just snapped. He'd hurt me and Dan, but that was the breaking point."

Izzy's eyes were shining. "Oh, Anna. . ."

"I'm OK," I said, not sounding very convincing.

"We're reporting him to the school. Me and you. He can't get away with this. It's harassment."

"I'm not sure—"

"No. You have to do this." Izzy gripped my hand. "Please? For me?"

I thought of all the times I hadn't listened to her, my best friend. I squeezed her hand back and nodded.

I had to do something.

*

I didn't think I'd see him so soon. I'd assumed he'd stay away, keep his distance. But as soon as I stepped out of art, I saw him waiting by the outside doors. Izzy was right behind me. I heard her sharp intake of breath.

"Ignore him, Anna," she whispered.

My stomach was in knots, but I made myself do it. I began to walk, trying to calm the burning in my cheeks and the shaking in my legs.

"It'll be fine," Izzy said, softly.

Except Will wasn't ready to let me pass. He stepped out in front of me, a smile pasted on his face. "Hey, Anna. Don't run off. We need to talk."

"She doesn't want to talk to you!" Izzy said.

"Seriously?" Will gestured at Izzy. "Are you going to let someone else do your talking for you? I thought you were better than that."

His words stung. "She's right," I hissed. "I don't want to talk."

"Are you mad at me?" His eyes went all big and innocent.

"Please, Will . . . move out of the way."

"It was just a joke!" He shrugged. "I don't know why you're making a big deal about it."

A small crowd had formed behind us now. People were staring. This was interesting.

"Some joke. You humiliated me," I said.

"You're scum," added Izzy.

There was a trickle of laughter and I saw Will flinch. "Babe ... don't be like this. It's just an argument. We can sort it."

I looked at him, like *properly* looked him at this time. His beautiful face, that wide smile, his big sexy eyes. But all I could see was a lost kid. Someone who threw a tantrum when he couldn't get his way.

Someone who hurt people.

"I don't want to," I said. "It's over."

Will tried to grab my arm, but I pushed him back. "Don't touch me."

"Now you're being silly."

"Silly? How would you like it if I took a picture of you – without you knowing? Posted it everywhere? How would you like that?" There was a murmur of agreement behind me. "You've gone too far this time. You've humiliated me. You're sick."

Will's cheeks were burning. He looked around and could see everyone looking at him. "You're out of order," he said.

"No," I said, feeling that last piece of rage exit my body. "You are."

The crowd cheered. And Will did the only thing

he was capable of doing: he went to grab me again. Except this time I was ready.

I took a quick sidestep and walked straight past him, shoving him slightly in the side as I moved by. He wobbled off balance and fell against the wall, swearing.

But I didn't stop. I kept moving as tears pricked my eyes, listening as the cheers engulfed the hall, wrapping him up in his own humiliation.

I hoped he choked on it.

"I'm so glad you're back," Debs said, smiling up at me. She had a subtle brightness about her that lit up the small room. Her perfume, slightly woody, was the same as before. It reminded me of Mum – why hadn't I realized that before? It was relaxing, familiar.

I sat back in the chair, letting myself unwind in the soft leather. My hands uncurling, my legs stretched out. "Thanks for squeezing me in," I said.

"I heard you've been going through a bad time. I thought you might need a session." Debs was looking at me with those sharp eyes, still reminding me of a rabbit, but softer somehow. I noticed the gentle curve of her neck, the bright pinkness of her lips, the way she seemed to move so effortlessly – like she was floating. "Do you want to talk about it?" she asked.

"About Will?" The thought drifted between us like a feather. "Maybe."

"You don't have to. . ."

"I don't think I've got my head around it yet." I stretched my fingers out. "I don't know why I let him get to me like that."

"Do you really not know?"

I paused. Outside rain was pelting against the window, a gentle rhythm. I remembered how much I'd thought I needed Will. How I thought I was better with him.

"I don't think I was happy," I said.

"Do you want to start with that?"

The image of Will was shifting now. In his place was Mum standing there, bags packed, leaving us. Dad shouting. Eddie sobbing. But why not me?

Why hadn't I ever cried?

"I want to talk about Mum," I said.

So I did.

It was weird how detached I felt afterwards, going home. I didn't want to be with anyone else, so I sat at the front of the bus. I had so much to think about. I didn't want anyone else bugging me.

My phone had buzzed on and off all day. Texts from Will. I deleted them without reading them; it was easier that way. I didn't want to hear his lame excuses. I didn't want to see any empty threats.

I'd spent lunch holed up in the music room, chatting with the band. Dan was talking of re-forming once his hand was better. I wasn't so sure. But I loved being in that space again, laughing.

Being me.

When a figure approached me on the bus, I flinched, got ready to get up and leave. But it was OK. It was Lyn.

He flopped down next to me, beaming. "Guess what! I got into sixth form here!"

I stared back; then the smile broke across my face. "Seriously, Lyn. That's amazing!"

"I know, I can't believe it. Jess was right. I must be a bit clever after all!"

"That's so good." But despite myself, I could feel my smile failing. I turned back to the window.

"Hey! You OK?" He poked me in the side. "Lately you seem so down. It's not like you."

"It's nothing," I said, my eyes heavy. "I don't want to go into it."

"Not that loser of a boyfriend, then?" he said quietly.

"He's not my boyfriend any more," I said, too sharply.

"Oh," Lyn said. "I'm sorry."

"Don't be sorry. It's fine."

At least it will be in the end...

We sat the rest of the journey in silence. Lyn was texting next to me, his leg jiggling. Obviously excited to tell everyone his good news. He got up at the stop before mine. "I'm meeting Jess," he said, grinning. "Going out to celebrate."

"Cool," I said, hating the twinge of jealousy I felt.

He grabbed the rail, ready to move. Then his head flipped back. A puzzled expression suddenly appeared on his face. "By the way, I do know your boyfriend, or more importantly I knew his brother."

"Jez?" I looked up. "Really? You knew him?"

Lyn was shaking his head softly. "Well – in truth I knew of him. A nasty piece of work. He used to hang around the Mac, wanted to be part of the crew," he snorted. "A posh little kid that didn't fit in, trying to look hard – pretty dangerous really."

"He ran away, didn't he? That's what Will told me."

"Like I said, he was nasty, real mean. Used to beat kids up for kicks – that sort of thing. I heard he hurt some kid real bad, over nothing. He just beat him at footie or something and Jez lost it. He smashed the kid's face up, broke his nose, left it a pulp. He was like that, would just attack people in rage. He never knew when to stop. Anyway, the kid was only thirteen. His brothers wanted to get revenge, so Jez disappeared. Rumour was he legged it to London, to some relative."

"What the hell. . ." I breathed out hard.

"Yeah . . . well, I guess it's messed with Will a bit."

"What? Because he's not come back?"

"Nah! Not just that. . ." Lyn said, his voice low.

The doors whipped open, cold breeze sweeping through the bus. I shivered.

"Those brothers caught up with him and beat him up worse. Far, far worse. They bashed Jez's head in." Lyn's expression softened. "He died, Anna. Four years ago."

School have called Dad. They tried calling Mum but she was out of her head again of course. School say I need help. They think my recent behaviour "indicates that I'm struggling to cope" with your death.

I think they're idiots.

So he's home again. It's all a bit awkward, to be honest, but he blames himself I think, because he ran away too. He's promised to stay with me now. We'll see...

He said he doesn't want me to be destroyed as well. I look at Mum curled up in her chair and I guess he has a point.

Was it worth it? Making everyone hate you? Having your head kicked in by some guy in a back alley? Was it worth it to die alone, in filth, everyone loathing you?

Was it worth it?

Maybe I do need to do something. Maybe there is another way.

Trouble is, I miss you. I miss my brother. Even though you treated me like scum most of the time, I loved you. You were everything I wanted to be. You weren't always bad, people forget that, even me. And now you're gone – there's a big hole. I keep being sucked into it. It's dark in there.

I want to cry but I can't. I never have. I wish I understood stuff. I wish I understood why you did that bad stuff to me.

But I'll never know now. I guess I have to learn to let it go.

This is my last letter. Tomorrow we are visiting your grave. We haven't been since ... well, you know.

My life has to stop being about you, Jez.

After

The lights fade up gradually, so bright I can barely see. Dan's guitar still reverberates beside me; the drums have reached their crescendo.

It is at that moment when it hits me again. I am flying. Energy buzzes through my arms, through my chest and out of my skull. My last note is high and loud. I let rip. Raw energy burns with it.

This is my song. A new one. All mine. Only I will really understand it.

A song about love. And control. And pain.

And Will. He should understand it too.

The applause is wild. It lifts us, sweeps us up in a wave of love and appreciation. Someone cheers, a wolf whistle. Dan runs to me, pulls me into a hug, so tight I can barely breathe.

"That was amazing," he screams into my ear.

I am beaming. I throw my arms up. I whoop. Jump about.

I am alive. I am free. I am me.

I squint out into the audience and I can see them. I can see Dad at the front, waving hard. Eddie is next to him. He sticks out his tongue at me, but I can see he's fighting a grin.

My eyes flick further back. I'm searching. Then I find her. I breathe hard. I can see her, I can see her so clear. She's four rows from the back. Her hair still tightly pulled in a bun, her eyes gleaming in the light. She is smiling straight at me.

"Mum," I whisper, and it's all I can do not to cry.

Mum...

And then I see him. He is sitting right at the back, slumped and small. He looks shrunken. A tug of something inside me. Pity? Sadness for what he destroyed? Something...

He looks lost.

I blink quickly and turn. Despite these feelings, the strength was always in walking away.

And I am strong now.

The truth is, I always was.

One bully. One target. Two victims.

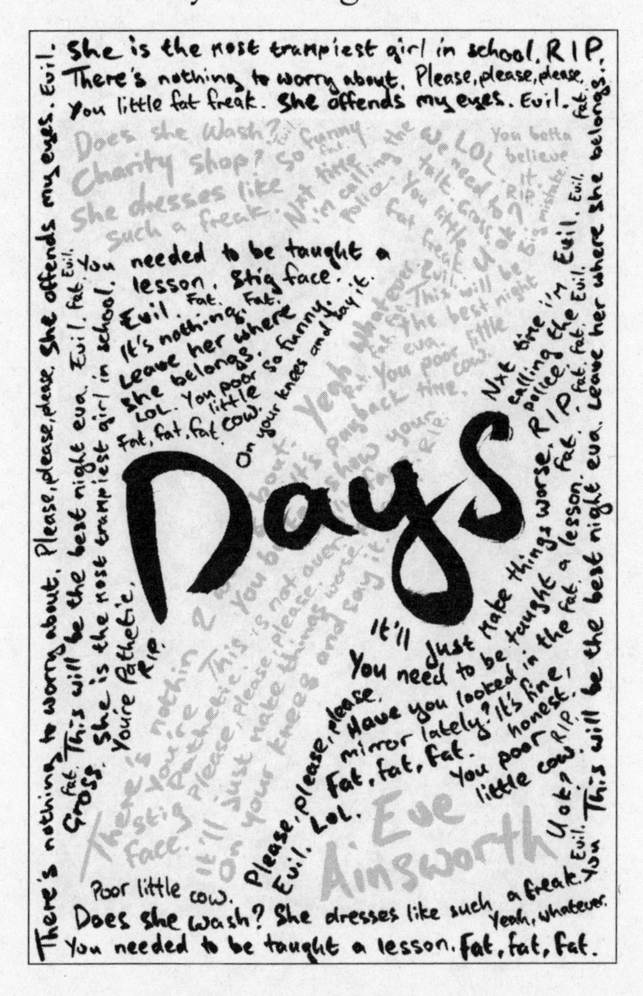

Read the powerful debut novel
from Eve Aisworth.

Eve Ainsworth has worked extensively in Child Protection and pastoral care roles, supporting teenagers with emotional and behavioural issues. She is also the author of Seven Days. Eve lives in West Sussex.

@EveAinsworth
www.eveainsworth.com